Changa's Safari
Volume II

A Novel By

Milton J. Davis

Mvmedia

Fayetteville, Georgia

CHANGA'S SAFARI
VOLUME II

A NOVEL BY
MILTON J. DAVIS

Mvmedia
Fayetteville, Georgia

ISBN Number: 978-0-9800842-2-1

Cover art, maps and interior illustrations by Duane Parker
Cover Design by Uraeus
Layout/Design by Uraeus
Edited by Lyndon Perry

Manufactured in the United States of America
First Edition

THE SAFARI CONTINUES
By Charles R. Saunders

Changa the traveler

In this second volume of Changa's Safari, Milton J. Davis's singular warrior-merchant continues his journey through both the familiar and fabled lands of late 15th century Africa and Asia, during the time before the centuries-old trading networks between those continents were permanently disrupted by incursions from Europe. However, Changa Diop is not merely a wanderer. He is also …

Changa the merchant

Arabia, India, China, East Africa, Japan and numerous other lands collectively labeled the "Mysterious East" by outsiders were awash with riches of all kinds, ranging from gold and precious gems to intricate carvings to magnificently woven textiles to succulent spices. Unlike many heroes of pure fantasy genres, Changa is not out to plunder the wealth of the Eastern lands. As an entrepreneur with his own ship and crew, he buys, sells, and trades, always looking to secure a profit. But even though he is a merchant, he is not an avaricious money-grubber. He is …

Changa the warrior

As a one-time slave who battled his way out of the East Coast fighting pits, Changa is a ferocious combatant either with or without weapons. Along with his companions – Panya the Oyo sorceress, Zakee the Prince of Yemen, Mikaili the Ethiopian navigator, and Sirocco the silent Tuareg swordsman – Changa often encounters circumstances that necessitate combat rather than commerce. Yet there is more to Changa than brawling and bargaining. For he is also …

Changa the seeker

Even as this new part of Changa's safari takes him through India, Arabia, and Ethiopia, the warrior-merchant is a hunted man – not by the law, but by the sorcerer who killed Changa's parents and caused him to be taken as a child from his native land of Kongo, deep in the heart of Africa and thousands of miles from the East Coast. Changa's enemy now wants him dead. And Changa, in turn, seeks to hunt down and eliminate his nemesis even as he endeavors to do what's best for his trading enterprise.

In *Changa's Safari: Volume II* Milton deftly combines history and mythology in a way that carves out new ground in the Sword and Soul genre. Changa is a complex character, and lives, fights, and loves in times that are interesting – but not in the ironic way implied by that oft-quoted Chinese proverb. Hard choices confront him at every turn – and sometimes he makes the wrong ones. He always tries to do the right thing, though.

The anchor is up. Wind is filling the sails.
Changa's safari continues.

To my sisters, Paula, Ivy and Debbie
Thank you for making my life an adventure…
and teaching me how to dance.

KITABU CHA NNE:
(BOOK FOUR)
KALI'S DAUGHTER

She sauntered onto the balcony and gazed into the darkness, a warm breeze teasing the ends of her sheer silk gown. The night was as black as her hair, the stars flickering like tiny torches in the distance. For the first time in her life she felt safe. Her raja promised he would protect her, and so far he had kept his word. The hunting mahal was one of his father's largest, a huge collection of elegant buildings surrounded by high thick walls and dense forests.

She turned to regard him, his naked body stretched out across the cushions, his brown skin glistening from the sweat of their lovemaking, his details obscured by the mosquito net. She did not love him but she was certain he loved her. It was easy for her to capture a man's heart. Her beauty attracted them like a bee to a brilliant flower and her ways made them promise all they could give. She wanted only one thing, protection. It was a gift every man was eager to give, but it was the one thing that never endured.

The sensation began at the small of her back, running up her spine to her head and emerging like fire in her eyes. She jerked her head around and ran to the balcony, her face distorted with dread, hoping she would not see what her senses warned. Scores of hands appeared on the edge of the wall followed by turbaned heads as the interlopers pulled themselves up. She stood frozen as they dropped into the courtyard one by one. Yells and screams rose to her ears and she answered with a painful howl.

The prince struggled up. "What is it?"

She ran to him, tearing through the mosquito netting, her eyes crazy with fear.

"They are here! They are here!" she screamed.

"What are you talking about? No one is here but us and my men."

"Thuggee! Thuggee!"

Terror flooded the raja's eyes. He jumped from the bed and ran across the room, grabbing his sword as the door crashed in.

The invaders gripped yellow scarves in their calloused

hands. They saw her and hesitated, then turned to the raja standing naked with his sword.

"If you leave now you have a chance to live," he said.

They attack him like starved wolves. The raja fought well, but they were too many. They dodged his swings and thrusts waiting for the right moment. One of them finally broke through his guard, slipping behind the prince and throwing his scarf around his neck. As the raja tore at the scarf another attacker ripped the sword from his hand and grabbed his feet. A third man grabbed the raja's head, snapping it forward as the second man pulled his feet away and the scarf wielder pulled opposite. They strangled him in seconds, dropping the body to the ground absently.

She watched her husband murdered and felt nothing. It was ending as it had before. Was there anyone one who could protect her?

They approached her and she backed away towards the balcony.

"Stay away," she whispered.

They fell to their knees in unison. One of them stepped forward, a gaunt man with a dense moustache and dark eyes. A dingy turban encircled his head, held together by a brilliant ruby pendant. He extended his hand to her, a reverent smile on his face.

"We have come to take you home, goddess," he said. "Please accept these sacrifices as our gift."

"NO!" she screamed. "Why can't you leave me alone?"

She stomped the floor and the room shook. The others lifted their heads, fear in their eyes. Their leader stepped away.

"Please, goddess, we do not mean to offend you."

The anger came from inside, coursing through her like a swollen river. Her skin darkened like the night sky, her pupils disappearing into a searing white glow.

"Why won't you leave me alone!" she hissed.

The men scrambled to their feet and ran for the door. She smiled, raised her arms, and danced.

1

THE SANGIR'S REVENGE

The wiry man ascended the towering palm tree with grace, rivaling the dexterity of the local primates. Upon reaching the upmost fronds he freed his spyglass from his waist belt then raised it to his eye. From his perch he could see for miles. The opposite shore of the strait was in full view; he waved at his cohort atop a similar tree on the opposite shore then turned his attention east to the mouth of the strait. His purpose was the same as it was every day. He searched the waters of the Malaccan Straits, seeking a particular group of vessels worthy of Sangir attention. Not every fleet carried the cargo that interested the *bajing loncat*, but this particular fleet was special not for the cargo it possessed, but for the men that sailed the collage of vessels. The men they sought were Sofalans and their leader was a man whose name raised fury in the heart of every Sangir: Changa Diop.

Changa stood on the deck of the *Kazuri*, patiently awaiting the word from the crow's nest. His simple cotton pants and shirt did little to distinguish him from the other baharia, though their deference to him revealed his status. His right hand rested on the hilt of his Damascene *shimsar* while his left hand shielded his eyes from the sun's glare. The Tuareg stood beside him draped in his blue robes, his *shesh* covering his face except for his intense brown eyes. Changa's silent cohort folded his arms across his chest, jostling the *takouba* resting in the worn baldric hanging from his shoulder. The man in the crow's nest climbed down to the deck, nodding to Changa.

"It is as he said," Nafari said. "They are waiting for us."

Changa chuckled. "That old fool was right. The Sangir apparently have a score to settle with us."

He patted his old friend's shoulder. "Well, let's give them their chance." Changa turned to the drummer at the stern and nodded. The drummer beat out a slow rhythm and the air rattled with the sound of rising anchors. The fleet eased into the straits, every man on deck and alert. Another group was on the move as well, a group of men led by Amir Zakee. They had landed on shore during the night, waiting for the signal from the *Kazuri* to proceed. The drummers' signal not only told them to march, but it also gave them an approximate idea of where the Sangir were hidden. Zakee signaled his companions with an exaggerated flourish of his scimitar, a proud smile on his face. Changa finally trusted him enough to give him an important command. Better still was the crew trusted him as well. When Changa announced the prince as the leader there was no limit to the baharia volunteering to accompany him. They moved swiftly along the banks, using trails when they found them, fighting their way through tangles of vines and brush when necessary, all the while keeping ahead of the approaching ships.

The *Kazuri* distanced itself from the other ships. Changa turned command over to Mikaili, the Ethiopian's skills far superior to his in such close quarters. Baharia climbed into the sails with their crossbows while those below loaded the cannons.

Changa stood at the prow. "Okay Sangir, show us what you've been doing for two years."

He was answered by the roar of cannons. Plumes of water circled the small dhow, dousing everyone on deck.

"Where are they?" Changa shouted.

The Tuareg hit him on the shoulder, pointed to the shore. The cannons fired again and smoke spat from the jungle.

"The guns are on the shore?" Salt water rained down on them again as the Tuareg spun him to the left. He saw smoke riding from that shore as well.

"They have us in a gauntlet," Changa growled. "Signal the Sendibada and the Hazina to come. Have the others stay back. We'll head towards the left bank. Zakee is aground on the right. Let's hope he can find those bastards before they learn how to aim."

Zakee and his men rushed through the jungle to the cannons' lair. They heard the guns first report and immediately knew the danger the fleet was in. The sound led them to eight guns manned by bare-chested Sangir hidden from sight by a woven net of vines. Zakee's eyes narrowed as he raised his scimitar over his head.

"Allah Akbar!" he yelled.

The baharia charged into the clearing. The stunned Sangir stood frozen until the young prince sank his blade into the chest of the nearest pirate. The other Sangir yelled and attacked swarming the baharia with sewars and rage, abandoning the cannons for a more immediate revenge.

"The guns have stopped firing on the left bank," Changa shouted. "Zakee must be among them. Concentrate fire on the right bank. Signal the Hazina and the Sendibada to go forward."

The *Kazuri* fired into the foliage. Treetops burst into wood and smoke, the cries of men following soon after. The bowmen focused on the sounds and fired volleys, adding to the unseen carnage.

"Changa!" Mikaili's voice was loud and urgent. "Look to stern!"

Changa rushed to the stern and cursed. A swarm of canoes filled with Sangir approached, covering the strait from shore to shore. In the center of the mass were five junks, cannons jutting from each side, the sails filled with archers.

Changa waved to the Tuareg. "Signal Zakee to return as fast as he can. Bring the Hazina, the Sendibada and the treasure junk to us. The others are on their own."

The Tuareg ran to the bow and the drums rumbled. Panya came to his side from below deck, summoned by the foreboding cadence.

"We could use the wind on our side," he said.

"I'll do what I can," she replied. She hurried to the bow, removing her herb bags as she ran. Changa concentrated on the approaching fleet, assessing the strength of each junk. His archers fired on the canoes, picking off the Sangir one by one. More bowmen emerged from below deck, carrying a weapon Changa procured during his journey through China. The Han called it chu ko nu, a crossbow configured to hold ten bolts instead of one, with a mechanism that allow the bowmen to shoot all ten bows in seconds. Each bolt had been dipped in poison concocted by Panya. The weapon was perfect for defending walls or ships. The crossbowmen lined the sides of the *Kazuri*, their weapons loaded. The same maneuver was being repeated on Changa's other dhows and the treasure junk.

Zakee and his men emerged from the jungle as the Sangir canoes surrounded the *Kazuri*. The bowmen began their barrage, thousands of bolts streaming into the canoes like lethal rain. So many Sangir tumbled into the sea their bodies blocked the approach of the others, making them easy targets for the other crossbowmen. The smart ones rowed away, leaving the little warship for their bigger brethren. They set upon the other dhows and junks in the fleet.

Changa cursed as the Sangir swarmed the other boats, but there was nothing he could do. There were too many; he had to concentrate on saving his own ships and crew. The *Hazina* and *Sendibada* drew closer slowly, the Sangir canoes closing despite the heavy fire from their archers. But the sails suddenly filled as a strong wind blew in from the direction from which they entered. Changa turned to stern and met Panya's smiling face. Her arms spread wide, she chanted to her orisha, Oya, and her orisha answered with the unseasonably strong wind. His ships pulled away from their pursuers.

The yells of the ship bound Sangir reached Changa's ears. An image popped into his mind, a vision of Taozhu harbor, the *Kazuri* surrounded by Woku ships as they battled to help the others escape. Changa pushed the doubt brought by the memory from his mind. They battled alone that day, their fate doomed by the errant cannon fire from Taozhu dragon cannons. This day his dhows would fight together.

The *Kazuri* made a dead run into the midst of the Sangir junks. Arrows and bolts whizzed by Changa's head as he maneuvered to welcome the Sangir boarders. Angry Sangir swung from the mast ropes, falling onto the *Kazuri*'s deck with sewars and swords drawn. Cannons roared and the *Kazuri* shook, baharia and Sangir stumbling with the impact of cannon balls against wooden hulls. Chunks of wood sprayed from the broadsides of the junks flanking the dhow, but the *Kazuri* pushed through undamaged. Changa lost himself in the midst of battle, his throwing knives long spent in the bodies of unfortunate pirates, his Damascus cleaving the unarmored interlopers with deadly precision. He caught a glimpse of the Tuareg running along the railing like an acrobat, cutting down men with his double blades. The deck swirled in a cacophony of ringing metal, crossbow fire and human cries. Changa fought not with skill but instinct, moving with the deadly skill of the pit fighter, each blow meant to maim or kill quickly and efficiently.

The onslaught ended. Changa stepped over bodies as he looked about reviewing the damage. He ignored the junks sinking around him, victims of the *Hazina* and *Sendibada*. The dhows sailed up unnoticed during the battle, taking position outside the skirmish and unleashing their cannons on the junks. Beyond the three the battle raged, the Sangir continuing their attacks on the smaller dhows and junks. Changa's little fleet continued to sail onward, the treasure junk lumbering behind them unscathed.

"Let's get her cleaned up!" he shouted to his crew. The baharia, exhausted from the fight, trudged to the task, tossing the Sangir overboard to the sharks. The wounded were tended to; the dead handled with the care they deserved. Changa plodded to the bow and sat, his eyes fixed on the west. He had his fill of the East, though he knew his victory would mean disaster for the next fleet sailing the straits. The Black Sultan had defeated the Sangir again. Luckily for the Sangir, the sultan had no intentions of sailing the Malaccan Straits again.

The quartet sailed away from the melee, the treasure junk cruising through the remains of the Sangir junks. Zakee caught up with the *Sendibada* and boarded. He lost a few men, but they were aboard. The crews watched anxiously as the other ships continued to battle the Sangir, some fending off the swarms easily, others succumbing to the overwhelming ferocity. They all wanted to help but they were too damaged. By sunset the onslaught had subsided. They survived the Sangir gauntlet but paid a heavy price. Most of the dhows were either captured or sunk, their sparse crews and light armor too little protection against the Sangir swarm. The Han junks faired much better with only the smallest ones sustaining irreparable damage. Changa's dhows had survived. The *Kazuri* suffered the worst damage since it bore the brunt of the fight. They let the remaining merchants sail on ahead as Mikaili guided them to a nearby landfall far enough away from the Sangir to be safe. There they tended to the wounded and made repairs before sailing on.

When they finally reached Calicut Changa and his crew were exhausted. Disappointment soon followed. The Han, desperate to return home through the straits before the Sangir recovered, dumped their merchandise on the Calicut merchants. Changa's cargo was almost worthless.

Changa simmered in his cabin, flanked by his disappointed cohorts.

"When will this safari bear fruit? I thought the Han were our friends!"

"I told you not to trust them," Mikaili replied. "They have no loyalty beyond their own needs."

Panya sat silently, looking down at the table. Changa waited for her to commit but she said nothing. His eyes lingered on her a moment longer before shifting to the ever optimistic smile of Zakee.

"I know this is a disappointment, and the Han seemed to have slighted us. But remember, they rebuilt the Kazuri, which played no small part in our run through the straits. Besides, are there not more trading cities?"

"Of course there are," Changa growled. "I was hoping to trade our cargo here and head directly to Sofala."

Mikaili rubbed his chin. "There are two cities which may make this delay worthwhile," he said. "In Ceylon, jewels spring from the ground like yams. The sultans at home would pay dearly for baubles to drape their wives and consorts. And in Goa we might find a few merchants willing to trade items to take to Vijyanagar."

Changa cut an eye at the old bahari. "I think you like to see me angry. You could have mentioned this long ago."

"You didn't ask," Mikaili replied.

"Then it's settled," Changa decided. "We will sail to Ceylon for jewels and Goa for whatever we find!"

2

A Friend in Goa

Goa greeted the Sofalan fleet with beauty and abundance. The natural harbor was fed by three rivers, reminding the baharia of Mombasa with its tall coconut trees leaning over white sand beaches. Changa felt a pang of homesickness looking at the busy haven. Brown skinned men in loincloths loaded and unloaded cargo from dhows of all types, a sign of a prosperous city. Mikaili stood beside him, his ever-present scowl mysteriously absent.

"What did I tell you?" he said. "You'll get your fair share here. Goa is the pipeline to Vijayanagar, and Vijayanagar is insatiable."

"Good. We can sell this cargo and make something out of this safari." Changa was anxious to get home. His adventures in China had left him weary but also expectant. Something was different inside him. For most of his life he had struggled with the fear of returning to his true home, afraid to confront the man who killed his father but also fearful he would fail to fulfill his promise to free his mother and sisters from captivity. Usenge stood out in his mind as an unbeatable foe and his tebos haunted him wherever he went. That fear waned like a setting sun, replaced by a confidence gained over his months away.

Zakee and the Tuareg joined Changa and Mikaili on deck.

"What a magnificent harbor!" Zakee exclaimed. "I see many of my brethren among these people, Tuareg."

Changa hadn't noticed the Arabs among the native folks but he wasn't surprised. Their reach was wide, from Mombasa to the Spice Islands. They were present wherever there was money to be made.

He looked about with disappointment. Panya had not come to the deck.

"I know a man here that can get us to Vijayanagar," Mikaili said. "He's an honest man and a good friend."

"It's been a long time since you've been here," Changa assumed. "Are you sure he's still alive?"

Mikaili laughed, emitting a hearty rumbled that surprised all three men.

"He's alive, I assure you. The day he dies the world will end."

Changa smirked. "I'm looking forward to meeting this man."

Changa, Mikaili, and Zakee took a boat to the beach. Mikaili grabbed the first unoccupied laborer he saw and spun him about.

"Where do I find Ahmed Shem?" he inquired.

The man's eyes widened. "Are you sure you want to know?"

"Of course. I'm an old friend."

The man grinned. "Then he will be happy to see you. You'll be the only friend he has in Goa."

"This doesn't sound promising," Changa commented.

Mikaili waved his hand. "Ahmed is a hard man to get along with. You either love him or hate him."

"That sounds familiar." Changa gave Mikaili a sideways glance.

"Your jabs will not prick me today, Mombassan," Mikaili grinned.

He looked at the laborer. "Take us to Ahmed."

The man put his hands on his sides and glared at Mikaili. Mikaili scowled and went for his coin bag.

"Does anyone do anything as a courtesy in this world anymore?"

Mikaili dropped a coin in the laborer's hand. The man grinned then turned to lead them.

"Allah be praised! You are alive!"

The trio and their guide turned towards the exclamation. A man ran towards them, his hands raised over his head in praise. Changa's hand fell on the hilt of his Damascus; the Tuareg's takouba rested at his side. The man ignored their threatening poses and rushed up to Zakee before falling to his knees and burying his face in the young amir's robes.

"It is you! I would not have believed it if anyone told me, but I see you with my own eyes. Amir Zakee lives!"

Zakee knelt to the man and lifted him up. Nervous curiosity ruled his face as he looked into the man's admiring eyes.

"Brother, it is obvious you know me, but I must admit I do not know you."

"You would not, Amir. I am but a lowly merchant. Aden is my home as it is yours. Though you would be pressed to find ten good men that knew my name, everyone in Aden knows the Flower of Yemen."

Zakee looked up at Changa, his face glowing. "He's from Aden!"

"We heard as much," Changa answered.

Zakee smiled and turned back to his new found friend.

"Tell me of Yemen. How are my father and my brothers?"

The man's face beamed solemn. "Though the image of our homeland burns bright in my mind, it has been some time since I've seen it. As for the sultan and your family, I have much to tell."

Changa laughed. "So all of you talk like bad poets!"

He patted Zakee's shoulder. "Stay here with your new friend. We'll visit Ahmed and meet with you when we return."

The Tuareg nodded, indicating he would stay with Zakee. Changa and Mikaili left the three together and followed Mikaili's hired guide into the streets of Goa. They worked their way through throngs of marketers, women dressed in brightly colored sarongs and dull burkas, men draped in turbans, some Muslim, others Hindu, all sporting facial hair from minimum to extreme. Elephants move through the crowds carrying heavy items and important people, adding to the press and the heat. Changa was following his companions when a strange sensation sent a chill despite the heat. Someone was watching him. He looked about casually among the strange faces but noticed no stares. Still his right hand sought his knife bag. There was no reason for him to suspect an attack in this place but he also had not expected a tebo in Mongolia. Usenge's reach was wide; he had to always be on his guard.

Their guide led them from the market to a street bordered by dilapidated stone buildings. A different crowd mulled here, a crowd of workers and beggars that either cleared the way or followed them with hands outstretched for alms. Changa felt a tug on his knife bag and instinctively grabbed the boy attempting to steal his knives. The ragged boy screeched in terror as Changa lifted him into the air. No sooner did Changa lift him did he realize the boy was a distraction for his cohorts. Their true target was his sword; Changa snatched the blade out before they could get a good grip.

"Get back!" he bellowed. He tossed the boy he held at his swarming friends and shook his sword.

"Changa, quit playing with those children," Mikaili exclaimed. "We have business."

"Playing? These urchins tried to steal my sword!"

Mikaili glared and Changa considered putting a knife in his forehead. Instead he reached into his shirt and took out a handful of coins. He tossed the coins over the boys' head and they ran off for the loot.

A few minutes later they stood before the home of Ahmed. Changa wasn't surprised that the home was more a hovel. This journey had often ended in disappointment. Mikaili seemed genuinely shocked.

"This is the home of Ahmed?" He grabbed the worker's arm and shook him.

"Don't play games with me! My friend is an evil man and will not hesitate to kill anyone that crosses him."

The man jerked his head about to look at Changa. Changa played along with Mikaili's threat, snarling as he raised his sword. The man dropped to his knees trembling.

"Please sahib, do not kill me! This is the house of Ahmed I swear."

"What is all this commotion?" a voice questioned from behind the battered mahogany door. "Go away. I told you ruffians before I have nothing. Nothing!"

"We are not bill collectors," Mikaili shouted. "It's your old friend, Mikaili!"

"Bah! Mikaili is dead. He was killed in the Spice Islands."

"There are some who wish that was true but God had been good."

The door creaked open to reveal one rheumy eye. "Mikaili! It is you!"

The door flew open and Ahmed Yazeed jumped into Mikaili's arms. The man was the size of a large child with pale skin pockmarked red. His thin arms gripped the old navigator like a savior.

"You have come to save me from these evil men!"

Mikaili struggled to separate himself from Ahmed. "I wish I could say that was my reason here, but it's not."

"But you are here from the dead!" he squeaked. "And you have brought a warrior with you as well."

"I was never dead, Ahmed," Mikaili explained. "And Changa is not a warrior. He is my employer."

Changa stepped toward Ahmed then stepped back. The man reeked.

"We have come for your help. We wish to sell our goods in Vijayanagar and we are told you know the way. Is this true?"

Ahmed's demeanor changed. Round fearful eyes became narrow calculating slits.

"I am a man with great debts. Any job I take on must pay me enough to repay those debts."

"I have no idea what you owe but I'm sure I won't pay you enough to clear them," Changa answered. "I'm giving you a chance to get a new start and maybe live a little longer."

Changa's eyes darted to the left. Four men walked briskly in their direction, their intent clear.

Ahmed saw the men and squeaked. He jumped back into his hovel and slammed the door. Changa turned to face the men as their guide chose the moment to run away. Mikaili's hand fell to his sword but Changa shook his head.

"No my friend. Stay clear of this. We might be able to talk our way out of this. I need you to translate my words if they don't speak Arabic."

The men marched up to Changa apparently not impressed by his size or demeanor. The smallest of the four stood before him, raising his head to look the Bakongo in the eyes.

"Stand aside," he ordered in Arabic.

"We have business with Ahmed."

"If you have business with Ahmed then you have business with me," Changa answered. "He is under my employ now."

The man looked Changa up and down. He glanced back at his companions. Their expressions remained emotionless.

"Our employer is a reasonable man. Pay Ahmed's debts and he is free to go with you."

"I have no intentions of paying his debts," Changa answered. "Once he returns he can settle his accounts."

"That is not acceptable!" The small man reached for his blade then screamed as Changa cut off his hand. Changa spun away from the sword swing of the closest man then threw a knife into the gut of the man behind him. The other two men stood motionless, their swords drawn, their faces locked in shock. The short man clutched his bleeding stump as he whimpered.

"Take your friends and go. Tell your employer he can collect his debt when Ahmed returns. Understand?"

The men nodded quickly. They gathered their comrades then rushed away. Changa was about to relax when he sensed someone behind him. He whirled, throwing knife poised then froze. A woman stood a distance away, her face covered by a dark veil, a hood covering her head. Their eyes met and he swayed. He thrust his arm out instinctively and steadied himself on the nearby wall. Changa shook his head, blinked, then look up again. The woman was gone.

Changa turned to face Mikaili. The Ethiopian looked puzzled.

"Changa, are you…"

Ahmed shoved Mikaili aside and pounced on Changa,

smothering him with his gratitude and his smell.

"Thank you, sahib! I am yours to command. Ask me and I'll lead you to the end of the earth!"

Changa pried the man free and pushed him away. "I don't want to go to the end of the world. I've been there. I want to go to Vijayanagar."

"And you will, sahib, you will!" Ahmed clambered back to his door, stopping briefly to wrap Mikaili in his odiferous hug.

The men traveled back in silence to the harbor. Mikaili and Ahmed chattered endlessly, catching up on old times. Changa walked behind them silently, the image of the mysterious woman lingering in his mind. He knew no one in Goa; he'd never visited the port. But the woman seemed familiar, as if he knew her from some earlier place. Could she be the paramour of some wealthy merchant who'd seen him in his other life in Mogadishu? Or maybe she was a former slave freed years ago who had once pleasured him? He shrugged as he tried to clear his mind. Best to forget her and focus on the job at hand.

They arrived back at the dhows at midday. They were in sight of the dhows when Changa spotted Panya running toward them. Her face was clearly distressed. Changa pushed past Mikaili and Ahmed and ran to her.

"What is it?" he asked.

"It's Zakee. Come!"

Changa ran behind Panya to the shore. Zakee stood beside the man he'd met earlier, his face more serious than Changa had ever seen.

"What is going on here?" Changa inquired.

Zakee stepped to Changa and bowed. "Bwana Changa, for many days I have served with you as a companion and a friend. You saved my life and in your presence I have learned much of life and this world. But the time has come for me to leave.

There was a quiver in the amir's voice as he continued.

"It seems my country is at war. I must go to fight with my father and brothers. I must go home immediately."

"I understand how you feel, Zakee, but you are a member

of my crew. We do not let one of our own face dangers alone."

Zakee smiled. "I understand, but I cannot ask you to risk your lives in such a way. I have no idea what awaits me when I return home."

"It will take time for us to leave," Changa stated. "Mikaili and I must travel to Vijayanagar to trade our goods. When we return we will set sail immediately for Oman."

"You don't understand, Changa. I must leave immediately."

"No prince, I don't think you understand. You cannot rush into this situation. As you say you have no idea what is going on. Goa is a trade city. Find out as much as you can while we are gone. This way we all will be well informed when we return."

Zakee looked at the Tuareg. The blue man nodded.

"So be it. I will wait until you return. In the meantime my brother and I will learn what we can from our other countrymen. Tuareg, will you help me?"

The Tuareg nodded.

Changa looked at Panya. Things were strained between them since China. She met his gaze but did not smile.

"I leave the dhows to you while I'm gone."

"Yes, Changa. Are you sure you don't wish me to accompany you?"

An image of the mysterious woman jumped in his mind, her head moving slightly from side to side.

"No. It is best you stay here. You might interfere."

Panya frowned. "Interfere?"

Changa stood dumbfounded. Was that what he said?

"I did not mean interfere. I need someone here with the dhows. Zakee will be running about and I need Mikaili to translate."

Panya looked at Changa with questioning eyes. "I will stay."

Changa set about preparing for the safari to Vijayanagar immediately. He gave Ahmed gold to purchase the equipment they required and to hire the manpower as well. Mikaili accompanied him to the marketplace to assist. Changa retired to the *Hazina*. No sooner had he put up his weapons did Panya appear.

"Changa?"

He stood and folded his arms across his chest.

"Are you all right?" she asked.

"I'm fine," he replied. "Why are you asking?"

Panya's eyes moved from side to side like a child searching for the right words to say.

"You said you didn't want me to interfere."

"I misspoke."

"No, it was more than that."

Changa shrugged. He was no longer speaking to Panya the companion. He was speaking to Panya, daughter of Oya.

"Oya is stronger here than in China," she said. "I sense many things here, many spirits and powers familiar and unfamiliar."

"What does that have to do with me?"

"I'm not sure. Be careful on your journey, Changa."

"I'm always careful."

Panya remained in his cabin, continuing to stare at him.

"Is there something else?"

"No...no, there is nothing else."

She hurried away. It was not what Changa wanted but he could do nothing to stop her. It had to be her decision, not his. All he could do is what. In the meantime he had business to take care of.

3

SHARMILA

"Changa, come look!"

Zakee's excited voice woke Changa from an unexpected nap. He staggered out of his cabin to the deck.

"What the devil is going on here?"

Zakee grabbed his arm and dragged him to the prow. "Look!"

Changa rubbed his eyes, opened them and focused ahead. A small army of men and elephants rumbled single file through the market, a grand sight even for folks used to the servile pachyderms. Ahmed and Mikaili each rode an elephant with the mahout, though Ahmed looked much more relaxed than Mikaili. He also noted that Ahmed had taken the liberty to purchase new clothes. The rags he wore earlier had been replaced by a wardrobe rivaling the most successful merchant, white cotton pants and shirt covered by a long silk robe. A bright red turban wrapped his head.

"Sahib!" Ahmed shouted. "We are ready!"

"Get the men to unload the cargo," Changa told Zakee. "We'll let Ahmed select what will sell best inland. The rest we will trade here."

Zakee nodded and went about his duties. Changa watched him leave, concern on his mind. The Tuareg took his place beside him and placed a comforting hand on his shoulder.

"I know he'll be fine until we return but I still worry. He'll be entering the hornet's nest for sure."

The Tuareg shrugged and Changa nodded.

"One issue at a time," he said.

Changa proceeded to the beach. Mikaili looked exhausted; Ahmed pranced about like a child.

"I hired the best workers I could find," Ahmed boasted. "These elephants are in prime shape and suited for the most delicate cargo. We also have enough remaining for provisions along the way."

Ahmed handed Changa the remaining gold and Changa nodded.

"Excellent. My men are unloading our ships. I will leave it up to you to select what merchandise will sell well in Vijayanagar."

"That will be easy," Ahmed replied. "The rajas of Victory City possess wealth like the oceans possess water. Their recent defeat of the Mughals stuffed their coffers even more. Your arrival at this time is most fortunate."

Changa kept a close watch on Ahmed as he perused the cargo. He had a good eye, selecting only the best of the materials for the journey. By nightfall the cargo had been sorted and stored, ready for travel the following day.

He was walking along the beach amongst his items when the newly familiar feeling crept up his back. Changa turned to see the same woman he spied before Ahmed's hovel. This time she did not run away or disappear. She came to him, veil clutched to her face, headscarf covering her head.

"Sahib, I wish a moment of your time," she said. Her voice was melodious like a song bird, full of strength and suggestion. Changa studied her body and liked what he saw.

"How can I help you?"

"I see that you prepare to take a journey. May I ask your destination?"

"Vijayanagar."

The woman's eyes clinched and Changa felt her discomfort. She opened her eyes again, the pain apparently gone.

"I'm sure a man of your wealth has many servants, but would you be interested in acquiring one more? I am as strong as most men and familiar with the foods of this land. I can prepare you meals…and your bed if you wish."

Changa was not sure if her last statement was a matter of fact or an invitation.

"As you say I have many servants but your offer is tempting. What is your name?"

The woman removed her veil and headscarf and Changa

gasped. Never before had he seen a woman so lovely. Thick black hair bordered her brown face, her oval green eyes staring intently into his. Her full lips reminded him of the women of Mombasa but her straight locks proved she was a woman of Goa. She smiled and he smiled back.

"My name is Sharmila."

"You are beautiful," he said.

Sharmila frowned. "If so then beauty is a burden I wish I did not carry. Beauty does not fill my stomach or bring me peace."

"It could," Changa replied.

"That is not the way I wish," she snapped. "I am sorry to bother you, sahib. I will be on my way."

"No, don't go. I will hire you. You will tend to my belongings and cook my meals. You will also lend help to the others as needed."

"I prefer to be in your company only, sahib. As you have seen, my appearance can be disconcerting to many."

"As you wish. Go see Ahmed. Take this with you." Changa handed the woman one of his throwing knives. "He will sign you on and give you your first day's pay. Once you are done board the Hazina"—he pointed at the dhow—"and ask for Panya. She will find you a place to sleep for the night."

"Thank you, sahib. Thank you."

The woman sauntered away and Changa blinked as if lifted from a trance. He didn't need a servant. He did well on his own. He started to chase the woman down and tell her he'd changed his mind but then she glanced at him over her shoulder, her face graced with a grateful smile. Hiring her was a selfish indulgence, he mused. He shrugged; it had been a long journey and he was due some indulgence. He continued his walk along the beach, though his mind was far from his work.

The next day began with a raucous rising of elephants and men. Changa rose from his cot and prepared for the journey. He inspected his chest to make sure all was ready and secured his extra weapons inside. He examined the payment chest as well. The iron strong box was filled with precious metals and jewels, universal currency throughout the trade lands. As he secured the lock on his strong box someone knocked on his door.

"I'm almost ready!" he shouted.

"Changa, open the door please." It was Panya.

Changa's curiosity was high. He was leaving for what might be days or even weeks. He opened his door expectantly and was greeted by Panya's scowl.

"Who is this Sharmila?" she spat.

"She is a woman I hired."

"Then fire her."

"I can't."

"Can't or won't?" Panya snarled.

"Won't." Changa snarled back.

Panya's mouth dropped as her eyes went wide. "You don't think..." A smile came to her face. "Yes you do. You think I am jealous. This has nothing to do with you. I sense something about her."

"I bet you do," Changa replied.

"Changa, please, take me seriously. This woman is not normal. I feel a power about her."

"What kind of power?"

Panya bit her lip. "I'm not sure. It could be something inside her or it could be something she possesses."

"A talisman, maybe?"

"It could be. I'm not sure."

"I have talisman. It's nothing to worry about. I have you to look out for me."

"I won't be with you."

Changa shrugged. "I'll be fine. I'll make sure Sharmila doesn't slip anything in my food."

Panya approached him, her face serious and from what he could discern, a bit worried.

"Please Changa, be careful."

"I will."

He touched her cheek and she looked away. "We must talk

when I return."

Panya nodded. "Yes, we must."

Baharia arrived for his gear, interrupting their moment. He followed them off the ship to the waiting elephants. Ahmed yelled and gestured about in Arabic, Hindi and Swahili, directing everyone to their proper place. In moments they were ready. He approached Changa and Mikaili.

"You will ride with me," he said.

Changa and Mikaili climbed onto the lead elephant and the safari commenced. The elephants were slow but steady as they paraded through the market, the outer buildings and then onto the road to Vijayanagar. Rugged mountains bordered the way, gradually diminishing into open fields of wild cotton and tall grasses. Changa looked down to see Sharmila walking beside his elephant. She kept her distance from the others, her nervous eyes darting back and forth from the caravan and the surrounding landscape. Changa was beginning to wonder if Panya's warning had merit. She was definitely not comfortable, as if she expected something to happen any minute. Then she looked at him and smiled. His doubts melted away. Panya was being paranoid as always and probably a little jealous despite her protests otherwise.

They camped that evening along a shallow river slicing through the flatlands. By the time Changa completed inspecting his merchandise Sharmila had set up his tent and prepared his meal. She sat patiently before him, a banana leaf of simmering food in her outstretched hands.

Changa took the leaf and she began to leave the tent.

"No, stay please," he asked. "I hate eating alone."

Sharmila returned. "As you wish, sahib."

Changa suddenly felt guilty. "You don't have to if you do not wish to. You're not a slave."

"I wish to, sahib," she smiled.

Sharmila made her leaf, her movements slow and seductive. She sat before him, placed her leaf down and prayed. They ate in silence, Sharmila's eyes fixed on her food, Changa's eyes on her. When she looked up Changa jumped like a boy caught spying.

"Where are you from, sahib?" she asked.

"Mombasa. Have you heard of it?"

"I have. It is one of the Swahili cities. Many goods come from the Swahili."

"Is Goa your home?"

Sharmila's smile faded. "It is for now. I am from many places."

Changa looked at his food and thought of Panya. He grinned.

"Is the food not to your liking, sahib?"

"No, it's fine. Very good actually. Someone told me to be wary of it."

"Panya?"

Changa laughed. "Yes, Panya."

Sharmila nibbled on her flatbread. "She looks out for you. Is she your woman?"

"No." Changa's response was more abrupt that he wanted. "She is a member of my crew."

"She is different from the rest of you. Is she a priestess?"

"Yes. She is daughter of Oyo."

Sharmila took on a thoughtful look. "What did she say about me?"

Changa sat down his leaf. "She says there is a power about you she cannot recognize."

Sharmila nodded. "She seems to be a special woman. Maybe you should listen to her."

Sharmila's statement fueled his doubts until their eyes met. Changa did not consider himself a perceptive man but he knew goodness when he saw it. Sharmila was a good woman. Of this he had no doubt.

"Are you familiar with Vijayanagar?" he asked.

"Somewhat. It is the capital city of Maharaja Deva Raya's kingdom. It is the richest city of the Hindus. Some say the heart of the world beats in Vijayanagar."

"Sounds like a wonderful place to make money," Changa surmised.

Sharmila's gave him a disapproving look. "Some would say so."

"You are not impressed by wealth."

"I have been close enough to it to know that it does not change those things that are most important."

"Wealth can change some things," Changa responded. "It can give you the power to right wrongs and take revenge."

"Is that why you are here?"

Changa shook his head. Why was he having this conversation? Sharmila was his servant. Once this safari was done she would be paid and be on her way. There was no reason for him to share his intentions with her.

"I am a merchant. I live to gain wealth. My reasons are my own."

Sharmila nodded and stood. "Is there anything else you require of me?"

"No." They looked at each other longer than they should.

"Good night, sahib," Sharmila said as she bowed.

"Good night, Sharmila."

He watched her leave his tent. Panya had been right. Sharmila did possess power, but it was not the type Panya perceived. It would hard for him to keep a distance between them. This would be a long safari.

4
THE PRESENT AND THE PAST

The caravan arrived at Vijayanagar on the cusp of a hot hazy morning. The City of Victory lived up to its name and reputation. A glut of common huts and dazzling stone homes clogged the narrow roads winding between rocky hills that served as much as protection as shelter. Huge temples challenged the hills in height and presence, their surfaces elaborately carved with images of the gods they honored. The markets glimmered with an overabundance of fruits, grains, and other provisions as its brightly colored patrons mingled about with the vigor of a proud people.

Changa swayed with the rhythm of his elephant, observing the grandeur of the city from above. Ahmed's beast lumbered beside his, the look on the merchant's face light and happy.

"What do you think, sahib? She is a grand city, is she not?"

"I'm impressed," Changa admitted. "The Maharaja's city is truly a jewel. Where do we sell our wares?"

"We have a ways to go yet. There is a market near the palace which is made for what we possess. What you see now is like a pebble compared to the mountain of wealth that awaits us."

Changa smiled. Culture did not change the boasting of merchants. He was about to answer when his attention was drawn below. Sharmila walked among the others, her face marred with a fearful look. The nervousness she displayed on the open road seemed full blown among the teeming crowds. Changa motioned for his mahout to slow.

"Sharmila," he called out. "Come."

Sharmila looked him with a mix of shock and fear. "No, sahib. I am fine."

Changa tapped the mahout's shoulder and his elephant halted then knelt. He extended his hand to Sharmila. She looked about nervously then climbed onto the beast. No sooner had it stood than she pulled her veil tightly around her face.

"Who are you hiding from?" Changa asked.

Sharmila's eyes widened before she answered. "Am I so obvious?"

"I've been many places and seen many people," Changa answered. "Clothes change, customs vary, but people are all the same."

Sharmila smiled with her eyes. "There could be one that feels I am still in his employ. If he sees me it may cause trouble."

"Don't concern yourself. Matters of money are easily settled."

Sharmila closed her eyes and bowed. "You are a good man, sahib."

"Call me Changa. I'm your employer, not your master."

They reached the main market, a sprawling mass before the walls of the royal compound. Ahmed used the elephant's bulk to his advantage, forcing his way to an area close to the palace walls. They unloaded the cargo, arranging everything to make it easy to see. Changa met Ahmed and Mikaili, a skeptical frown on his face.

"So we just sit here and wait for a palace agent to show himself?"

"Exactly," Ahmed nodded. "See my flag?" He gestured to a white banner with a pair of open hands stitched into the center. "I am well known among the raja's servants. Someone will come to us soon. Of this I am sure."

Changa looked at Mikaili and the old navigator shrugged. "We have trusted him this far. We might as well trust him all the way."

Not long after their conversation a small crowd emerged from the palace, colorfully dressed and noisily announced. The group surrounded a large elephant draped in silk and jewels, its tusks capped with golden crowns. An equally ornate carriage followed, its carriage occupied by a bearded man dressed in fine silks, a serious look on his face. The elephant lumbered to Changa's camp, halting before the three leaders. It knelt and its important passenger climbed down to meet the men.

He stood before Ahmed. "Ahmed Yazeed, I thought you would be dead by now."

Ahmed bowed deeply. "I am alive as you can see, sahib Denesh."

Denesh looked at Mikaili and Changa, his eyebrows rising when he looked upon the Bakonga.

"I see you bring esteemed guests with you."

"Yes, sahib. This is my friend, Mikaili, and this…"

"Is Changa Diop," Denesh completed. He bowed deeply. "The Black Raja has come to Vijayanagar."

Changa was no longer surprised by his recognition but he was impressed that his false reputation had reached a land he'd never intended to visit.

"Thank you for suffering us," Changa answered. "We have traveled far to stand before you."

Denesh laughed. "Far indeed. Your goods reflect your journey."

He barely glanced at Changa's goods. "The raja will purchase it all."

Two men staggered forward carrying a large iron box between them. They sat the box down and opened the lid. A wealth of jewels gleamed at them.

"Will this be sufficient?"

Changa was stunned silent. Ahmed eyes widened.

"Yes!" Ahmed squealed. "It is…"

"It is sufficient," Changa interjected, his composure returned. "I thank the raja for his generosity."

"You can thank him personally," Denesh said. "The raja wishes your company tonight. He would be greatly disappointed if you refused."

Changa knew better that to refuse an invitation from a king.

"We are honored, Denesh. Does you invitation include my entire party?"

Changa glanced at Sharmila as the woman hid behind one

of the elephants.

"The raja's table can only accommodate those of the highest rank. Arrangements will be made for the others."

Changa bowed. "I look forward to meeting the raja."

Denesh returned to his elephant. No sooner did the beast rise than his entourage swarmed Changa's camp, procuring his goods for the raja. The site was empty in minutes.

Ahmed jumped about and clapped his hands. "See Mikaili? I told you Allah smiles on this safari!"

Changa knelt before the chest and ran his fingers through the treasure. He smiled, warmth cascading him like never before. This was the wealth he sought. With this he could raise an army in Swahililand. With this his return to the Kongo was assured.

The reality of their sudden wealth settled on Changa. They would need a safe and secure place for the night. Many of his men were with him but he would need more guards to protect them, guards they could trust. He would also have to hire more guards to accompany them back to Goa. His windfall was beginning to seem more a burden than a blessing with every moment passed.

"Ahmed, where can a wealthy merchant find lodging in this city?"

"Come with me, sahib! I know just the place."

Ahmed led them away from the palace grounds to an area of the city equally splendid for spiritual reasons. They passed between tall temples, their facades crowded with animated carvings. On the other side of the temples stood a building Changa assumed was a hostel.

"This is the safest place in the city, sahib," Ahmed explained. "It is close to the temples which discourages criminal acts. We can make offerings to the monks and they will supply us with guards for the night."

"I want to rent the entire building," Changa said.

"That's a foolish waste of money!" Mikaili exclaimed. "Even an old pirate like me wouldn't throw away jewels like that. It's like the raja gave you a bag of rice."

"I'd rather run a few patrons from their rooms thinking

they knew what wealth we possess than let them stay and remove doubt."

He turned back to Ahmed. "Take the owner this." He handed Ahmed a huge ruby. "Tell him there's another for him if we can have his hostel for the next two nights."

Ahmed hurried into the hostel flanked by two of Changa's baharia. Moments later irritated customers streamed from the building flashing angry eyes at Changa and his group. The owner was on the heels of the last evicted customer, waving his hands and cursing as he shooed the man away. His demeanor quickly changed as he hurried to Changa.

"Welcome to the Gandhali!" he said. "I am Prakal. Welcome to Vijayanagar."

A swarm of servants gathered their belongings and led them inside. The Gandhali was a modest place but sufficient for a short stay. The servants lead Changa away from the group to the rear of the inn.

Prakal appeared before him. "This is my best room, sahib. You will find nothing more inviting outside the raja's palace."

He opened the doors and Changa was indeed impressed. Whatever Prakal saved on the other modest rooms he spent on this room. Sharmila gazed into the immense room with little emotion.

"You are not impressed?" Changa asked her.

She shrugged her shoulders. "It is as I told you before, Changa. Wealth does not change what is most important. You will be comfortable here for only a night then it will be gone from you mind."

"You will stay with me," Changa announced, trying his best to hide the nervousness in his voice.

"Of course," Sharmila replied.

No sooner had they settled into their room did servants file into the room, filling the bath with steaming water. Changa undressed and bathed, thankful for the soothing distraction. Sharmila watched him intensely, whether from pleasure or duty he did not know nor did he care. He felt comfortable around her despite their short time together. There was something mysterious about her, the way she searched about as if being followed but still exposed to the others. He would have to find out the reason behind her strange behavior.

Changa barely finished his bath before the door opened again. A male servant entered, frowning at Sharmila before approaching Changa.

"Sahib, the raja wishes you to wear these garments."

Changa looked over the clothes and nodded. "I'll need something for my servant as well."

The man glared at Sharmila for a moment but then his expression changed to acceptance.

"As you wish. A woman as lovely as her will be greatly appreciated at the banquet."

The servant rushed away and returned quickly with garments for Sharmila. He handed them to her then quickly exited the room.

"I am almost done," Changa said. "I will give you your privacy…"

Sharmila had discarded her clothes. She stood naked before him, lingering as if awaiting his approval. Then she sauntered to the bath and entered the water slowly. Changa watched mesmerized as she bathed. She climbed from the bath and strolled back to the new clothes. Changa stepped toward her and her eyes narrowed.

"Not yet," a voice said in his head. *"I must be sure you are the one."*

Changa obeyed. Sharmila donned the clothes. She was as beautiful as any princess he beheld, even Panya.

"I am ready, Changa," she announced.

They met the others outside the inn. Everyone was resplendent in their new clothes, even the grumpy Mikaili. He tugged at his sleeves and pants then struggled with his turban.

"I never did like Hindu garb," he groused. "I don't see why…oh my!"

He looked dumbfounded at Sharmila. Changa felt unexpected pride at his response. Ahmed ran up to them and bowed deeply.

"It seems we had a diamond in the rough among us," he observed. "Hold on to this one tight, sahib. There will be princes and kings willing to part with much to claim this prize."

Ahmed's words seemed to upset Sharmila.

"Ahmed is right," she said. "I will wear my veil. We don't want any tension between you and the raja's own."

She wrapped her veil around her face. The group mounted their elephants and traveled to the palace gates where they were met by the Captain of the Guards. The gruff man looked them over, paying special attention to Changa. He huffed then signaled for the gates to open.

The House of Victory reflected the opulence of the city and the power of the Deva Raja. They passed through room after room of wealth, finally arriving at the waiting room for lesser dignitaries. Changa's group drew the close attention of the others; they were obviously not of the city and were truly newcomers to this daily ceremony. The doors eventually opened and the guests streamed in. Changa's group was guided to an area close to the raja.

"This is not good," Mikaili said.

"On the contrary my friend, this is excellent!" Ahmed smiled. "We are given a place of honor."

"But why?" Mikaili worried his beard. "A place of honor beside a king is a snake pit of obligation."

No sooner was Changa's group seated did Denesh appear from the crowd dressed more gaudily than when he first greeted Changa. He bowed respectfully to the raja and the others of rank. He gave a special bow to Changa. The look on his face made Changa wary.

"Mikaili, for once your instincts may be right," he whispered.

"Nobles of Vijayanagar, we feast for the victories that have come our way and the blessings the spirits have showered upon us. Today is a special occasion, for a great man has come to share honor with our raja. He has sailed from the Swahili Coast to the Land of the Ming and now comes to our sacred country. Welcome the Black Raja, Changa Diop!"

The nobles clapped and Changa stood, bowing respectfully to them all. He was about to take his seat when Denesh spoke again.

"The Black Raja's recent deeds are truly magnificent, but victories began long before this time."

"No," Changa hissed as a sly smile came to Denesh's face.

"Before he was the Black Raja, he was known in the fighting pits of Mogadishu as Mbogo!"

"That bastard!" Changa's clenched his fists.

Denesh was smiling full. "In honor of our raja, Changa has agreed to display his talents against our greatest champion, Jagajeet Bangalore!"

The room erupted in cheers and handclapping. Drums rumbled from the dining hall entrance as women danced into the room and cavorted along the perimeter of the open area. As the last woman danced away, Jagajeet Bangalore, Champion of Vijayanagar, entered.

He was an enormous man, at least a foot taller than Changa and twice as wide. He was naked except for a small loincloth. He raised his hands and the diners cheered louder. Changa was not impressed. He'd fought men like Jagajeet before, men who thought their size would conquer any challenger before them. The trick to defeating the champion of Vijayanagar would be doing so without killing him.

Changa stood as Denesh came to his side.

"I'm not pleased with you right now," Changa said.

The man smiled apologetically although Changa knew it wasn't sincere.

"Forgive me, raja, but when I saw who you were I couldn't contain myself. I saw you fight many years ago in Mogadishu and it was a battle I'll always remember."

"I was a slave then," Changa snarled.

"And look how far you have come! It is the honor of all honors to fight before the raja. You will lose, of course, but at least you will have a chance to display your talents one more time."

Changa's glare did not seem to faze the raja's servant.

"What are the rules of this farce?"

"They are simple. Three falls; a man concedes when he is thrown on his back."

Changa stepped out into the circle but Denesh stopped him.

"You must take off your clothes."

Changa shoved Denesh away and began to disrobe. Sharmila came immediately to his side to assist him.

"You can defeat this man," she whispered.

"We'll see."

"*When you do, what you saw before will be yours. You will be the one.*"

Changa looked at Sharmila, his heart racing. She moved her veil enough to show her smile.

Changa stripped down to his undergarments. The drummers formed a circle around the fighters, beating out a rhythm that stirred the crowd. Changa and Jagajeet approached each other and grasped hands.

Changa's vision blurred. He saw the ceiling for a second then grunted as his back slammed against the ground. His eyes cleared and he looking into Jagajeet's grinning visage.

Changa came to his feet amongst the cheers of the Hindus. Jagajeet was incredibly fast for a man his size. Changa cursed himself; he had underestimated his opponent, a failure which would have cost him his life in the pits.

The cheers died down and the two men grasped each other again. Jagajeet jerked Changa toward him and Changa followed. He shoved his right leg between Jagajeet's feet then slammed his forearm into the big man's chest. Jagajeet tripped over Changa's leg then stumbled backwards. He was about to regain his balance when Changa ran up to him and swept his feet away. Jagajeet crashed onto his side then Changa fell on top of him, rolling him onto his back.

The baharia roared; the Hindu response was polite but subdued. Changa and Jagajeet met one last time before the onlookers. Jagajeet stared into Changa's eyes. Changa smiled at the huge Hindu. The drums sounded and Changa jerked the massive man toward him as he squatted. Jagajeet fell over onto Changa's shoulders. Changa let out a grunt and lifted Jagajeet off the ground then dropped his shoulder. Jagajeet rolled off his shoulders and slammed into the ground. Changa dropped his elbow into his chest and the Hindu wrestler whooshed air. Changa then flipped him onto has back as he gasped for breath.

The stunned crowd was silent as Changa strolled to his clothing. Sharmila met him, her face unveiled.

"You are the one," her eyes read.

The raja stood and clapped enthusiastically and the Hindus followed suit, though their expressions revealed their displeasure. Changa grimaced as he sat, his pain subdued by Sharmila's attention. Denesh came to Changa with a nervous smile.

"Forgive my deception," he said. "When I recognized you my heart jumped with joy. I thought only of how the raja would be pleased to see you fight. I did not consider your feelings."

"And was your raja pleased?" Changa asked.

Denesh smiled. "Yes, very much."

Changa's right hand shot out like a cobra strike, slamming into Denesh's groin. The man's eyes rolled back and he collapsed before Changa. The room burst into laughter.

The raja's servants gather their companion. One of the servants stood before Changa and motioned toward the raja. The monarch waved at Changa.

"I think you're being invited to join him," Mikaili whispered.

"It is a blessing!" Ahmed shouted. "The gods continue to shine their blessings on me."

"I guess I should go," Changa decided. "Sharmila, come with me."

This time there was no shocked look on her face. She stood with Changa and followed behind him to the throne of the raja. They followed the servant to the raja's throne, the nobles looking upon them with shocked and curious expressions. One noble's expression was different from the others. The bearded man looked not at them both, but at Sharmila. His expression was one of hatred.

"*Namaskar*," the raja says, his hands pressed together. Changa repeated his gesture.

"I apologize for my Arabic," the raja said fluently. "I usually use it in anger."

"I am honored by your invitation." Changa and Sharmila sat beside the raja. The raja's eyes lingered on Sharmila before returning to Changa.

"Jagajeet had never been defeated until today," the raja revealed.

"Every man suffers defeat one day," Changa answered.

"They say Mbogo was never defeated. Your record stands."

"It is nothing I am proud of. I gain no pride in something I was forced to do."

"It was your karma. I'm sure it is because of your skill that you sit before me with a fortune for your goods."

Changa could not argue against the raja's logic but he would much rather be sitting before a living father in Kongo than a foreign king and a strange but alluring woman.

"Why have you come to my city?" the raja asked.

"I was told Vijayanagar was a city of great wealth and there would be need for my cargo. It's seems that was good advice."

"Again your karma is good. Are you truly the Raja of the Swahili?"

Changa laughed. "No. The Swahili have no raja, sultan or king. That story was one spread by the Ming eunuchs for their own reasons. It follows me like the rains."

"I am not so sure they were wrong," the raja argued. "Some men are born with rank; others achieve it by their skill and valor. I sense nobility in you, Raja Diop."

"I am but a merchant," Changa replied.

The raja grinned. "Well merchant, thank you for your cargo and your skills. I am pleased. You have my protection as long as you choose to stay in my kingdom."

The raja removed a large ruby ring from his finger and extended it to Changa. Changa's eyes widened. This was no rough cut jewel. It gleamed in the light, a stone obviously cut to perfection for a king. It was easily worth more than the jewels which paid for his cargo.

"Thank you, Raja."

The raja grinned and turned his attention back to the feast. Changa enjoyed a constant flow of exquisite delicacies, each meal more sumptuous than the last. Sharmila ate daintily beside him, constantly glancing at him and smiling. His appetite for food diminished, replaced by a more urgent hunger. By the end of the feast Changa's full attention was on Sharmila and hers on him.

"Changa. Changa!"

The merchant tore his eyes away from Sharmila to Mikaili's smirking face.

"Quit making a fool of yourself. The raja left over an hour ago and you didn't even notice. Everyone is expecting you to take this woman in front of us all."

"Raja Changa will reside in the palace tonight," a voice cut in.

Changa looked up to see three burly guards surrounding a small servant with an arrogant smile.

Changa stood before the servant. "I will be honored."

Mikaila's look betrayed him. "Do you think that is wise?"

Changa shrugged and looked at Sharmila. "Is it?"

"You are under no obligations to stay," she explained. "Although the raja would feel slighted if you refused. I think it would be best that you do, if even only for the comfort and the company."

Changa could tell the company she spoke of had nothing to do with the other nobles.

"I think you have your answer." He patted Mikaili's shoulder. "I'll be fine. If not, you'll be a rich man."

"In that case I hope the worst for both of you." Mikaili smiled then went away with the other baharia.

They were about to follow the raja's servant when the man Changa noticed earlier stepped before them, flanked by two armed cohorts. He ignored Changa, his eyes locked on Sharmila.

"How dare you come here!" he spat.

Changa stepped before the man, shoving him away.

"Who are you?" he asked.

The man's eyes went wide. His men moved toward Changa but his sword tip was at the man's throat before his men could draw steel.

"I ask you again, who are you?"

"He is Raja Damudar Rana," Sharmila answered.

"What is he to you?" Changa asked.

"I was married to his son," she said. "He was killed on our wedding night by Thuggee."

"So you say," Damudar replied.

"I am sorry for your loss, Raja," Changa said. "This woman is in my employ, which means she is also under my protection."

The raja's servant stepped forward. "Damudar Rana, do you threaten the guests of the raja?"

"Don't play dumb, Ajeet!" Damudar shouted. "You know what is going on. If the raja knew…"

"He does know," Ajeet said. "As I said, these people are under the raja's protection."

Damudar glared at Changa, then at Sharmila.

"I know where you are now, woman. I know where you are."

Damudar and his men stalked away.

Sharmila's shoulders dropped and she exhaled.

"Changa, I..."

"Don't explain," Changa said. "We all have our secrets. Come, Ajeet awaits." Changa and Sharmila followed the servants into the main palace.

The servants led them down an opulent hallway to a dwelling that was more a small palace than a room. No sooner had the servant closed the door did Sharmila jump into Changa's arms.

"There have been many before you, Changa," she declared between kisses. "They told me they could protect me but they failed. If I had looked beyond their words I would have seen the truth. But I see your truth. You can protect me. You will protect me."

Changa was overwhelmed by Sharmila's passion. Something was wrong, he was sure, but it did not matter.

"What am I protecting you from?" he managed to ask.

Sharmila pulled away from him, an expression on her face which was sad yet sensuous.

"From myself," she whispered.

5

THUGGEE

Changa's inconspicuous merchant trip had become an extravagant parade courtesy of the raja. When he and Sharmila emerged from the palace they were greeted by a team of elaborately decorated elephants and an army of additional servants. Standing before them was a subdued Denesh. Changa's face became stern and he picked up his pace. Sharmila touched his arm.

"Wait, Changa. I think Denesh has something to say."

Denesh came to Changa and bowed deeply.

"Raja Diop, please accept my forgiveness. I thought the raja would be pleased by your skills and I did not realize you would be offended by such a display."

"You were right on one account," Changa growled.

"The raja offers his travel tent for your comfort during your return to Goa. He has ordered that I serve you during your journey."

"I would rather beat you senseless, but I'll accept your service. Get your crew together. We're leaving immediately."

The Swahili set off for Goa. Changa and Sharmila shared an elephant despite the abundance of the beasts supplied by the raja. It was good to be close to her, to feel her warmth against him. His mind shifted and a twinge of guilt took him as he thought of Panya. They had come close as well in China but the Yoruba princess had erected a wall between them stronger than the platonic one that existed before. He had tried to breech it but her resistance held firm. Now the feelings he had for Panya were fading.

"You are thinking of her, aren't you?" Sharmila said.

"Who are you talking about?" Changa replied weakly.

"The beautiful princess," she said. "Panya."

"I am," Changa admitted. "We became close in China. Since then she has chosen to take our relationship as it was before. It is her right. I will not challenge it."

"Yet you're not happy," Sharmila challenged.

"As I said. It is her choice."

"And what of me?" she asked. "Is it my choice?"

Changa slipped his hands around Sharmila's waist. "When we reach Goa I will board my dhows and return to Sofala."

"Then I will return with you if you ask."

Changa was startled. "Are you sure?"

"As you said, Raja. It is my choice."

They camped in a clearing of cotton and grass for the night. The jagged mountains of Vijayanagar were still in view, the full moon pouring its muted glow over the peaks and fields. Denesh orchestrated the set-up of the raja's tent as Changa, Mikaili, and Ahmed looked on.

"A damn waste of time," Mikaili snarled. "You can sleep on the ground like the rest of us."

Changa chuckled. "I wouldn't want to insult the raja, now would I?"

"And an insult it would be," Ahmed added. "To refuse the raja's gift would say that what he offered was beneath you. This raja is a fickle one. You do not want to be on his bad side, as the Mughals have discovered."

Changa's attention drifted to Sharmila. She trailed Denesh as he shouted orders to the workers. Occasionally she would lean close to the man and whisper into his ear. He would nod then shout more orders.

"And what of her?" Mikaili asked.

"She's the finest jewel of them all," Ahmed sighed.

"She's been an excellent servant," Changa said.

"Servant my..." Mikaili touched the cross dangling from his neck. "Your relationship has gone far beyond work. What will Panya think?"

"Panya made a decision before we left China. She has held to it."

Mikaili shrugged and rolled his eyes. "This is why I decided to be a priest."

Changa's palatial tent was complete by nightfall. The

other men had set up tents as well, the darkness punctured by flickering campfires. Changa strolled through the camp chatting with his companions and inspecting the merchandise. This wealth was far beyond his expectations. Though his success in China was modest considering the distance and efforts traveled to procure it, his windfall in Vijayanagar more than made up for the shortfall. Sharmila met him as he returned to the tent, dressed simply in a loose blue shirt and billowy cotton pants. She grasped his hand and led him inside the tent. The interior was as plush as a room in the raja's palace, the air scented with pungent incense. A large porcelain tub occupied the center of the tent, tendrils of steam rising from the heated water inside.

Sharmila began stripping off his clothes. "You must bath before we begin."

Changa shed his garments and scrambled into the tub. Sharmila looked at him, a sly smile on her face.

"Aren't you coming in?" he asked.

"No." Sharmila raised her arms over her head. "I will dance for you."

Her hips swayed and Changa's attention was captured. She moved languorously, the rhythm of her steps matching the pace of his heart. Changa had been privy to many such displays; his profession required he spend many nights before vigorous dancers and equally vigorous business partners. He would never indulge in the expense alone for he thought himself above such baser pleasures. As she twirled sound melted away, his heart beat prominent in his ears. The tent filled with darkness; Changa's eyes beheld only Sharmila and her sensual dance. Her clothes fell away, revealing golden strands of jewels clinging to her skin and accenting her curves. Her dance became more vigorous as her skin transformed from golden brown to deep black. The jewels and metals sparkled with her energy. His heart beat faster and Sharmila kept pace. Changa stood absently and climbed out of the tub, water steaming off his hot skin as he approached Sharmila. Her sensual countenance transformed to a tense mask as she danced faster. The room spun, Changa and Sharmila at the center of a cosmic dance.

"Thuggee! Thuggee!"

Changa blinked and was showered by a wave of chaos. Sharmila collapsed onto her pile of clothes, her face twisted with malevolence.

"Why don't they leave me alone?" she shouted. "Why?"

The tent flap flew open and Mikaili stormed inside, a bloody sword in his hand.

"What the hell are you waiting for?" he growled. "We're under attack!"

Changa rushed by Sharmila to his clothes and weapons.

"By whom?"

"I have no idea," Mikaili barked. "Our men are holding but these damn Hindi are useless. They're yelling and running like a bunch of children."

Changa and Mikaili ran into the night. Shadows darted back and forth, illuminated by the fire. The baharia had gathered at the main tent, weapons at the ready. Denesh and the raja's servants were there as well but it was obvious by the terrified looks on their faces that they would be of no use. Elephants trampled through the camp, trumpeting their fear as they destroyed the smaller tents. The chaos edged slowly toward the tent; Changa heard a familiar and ominous sound among the din.

"Lances and bows!" he shouted. The men responded rapidly, the lancers taking position before the bowmen. The reason for Changa's hasty order charged from the darkness seconds later. Large maneless felines with black and orange stripes attacked them from all sides. The baharia held their ground. There was no panic in their eyes, only determination. They had sailed long with Changa and experienced many challenges that would cower the average man. These felines did not sway their bravery.

The first cats impaled themselves on the lances. The others halted, slapping at the spear points as they looked for gaps in the deadly line. The archers took advantage of the hesitancy, firing arrows into the beasts and bringing them down one by one. Changa paced back and forth making sure his men were standing true. A tiger slipped past a group of men and attacked them from behind.

Changa snatched a throwing knife from his bag and let it fly. The blade sliced into the tiger's side and the cat spun in his direction. He threw a second knife and it struck the cat between the eyes. It collapsed where it stood.

Changa ran to the dead beast and snatched his knives from the carcass. He glanced at the tent and stopped. Shadows struggled against the fire. Sharmila was not alone. He ran to the tent and charged inside.

Sharmila struggled with a strange man. The man was tall and lanky, his sinewy muscles taut and sweating. He wore a green loincloth that matched the turban wrapped around his large head. Two other men lay prostrate on the ground, their arms folded on their heads. By the looks on Sharmila and the intruder's face Changa knew they were familiar with each other.

"Why do you continue to deny your destiny?" the man pleaded. "We only wish to raise you to your proper place."

"Leave me be!" Sharmila screamed back. "I don't want your place or your worship!"

"You cannot deny what the gods have given you," he said. "It is your karma!"

Sharmila managed to break his embrace and shoved him away. The man's hand struck her face. She collapsed before him.

"I am sorry, goddess," he said.

Changa hurled his knife. The man's head jerked in this direction, his mouth twisted and his eyes narrowed. Then he was gone and the knife passed through nothing. Changa's senses alarmed him but he was not fast enough. He managed to grab the red cloth with his free hand before it tightened around his throat. The man who stood before Sharmila now stood behind Changa, pulling a silk scarf to his neck with strength far beyond his appearance.

"You will die like the others, you black dog!" he snarled.

Changa dropped his sword and gripped the scarf with both hands. His hands pressed into his neck, blocking the scarf from digging deeper. Still, his breath was constricted, the scarf tight like a python. He and his attacker struggled in a deadly stalemate with Changa's fingers slowly pulling the scarf away.

"My brothers, help me!" the man shouted. The prostrate figures leaped to their feet and ran towards the duo. Changa fought harder as he realized what they planned to do. They would lift his legs, using his own weight to aid in his strangulation. Changa waited until they were bending for his legs when he kicked out with both feet, striking the men in their necks. They reeled away as he fell to the ground, jerking his upper body forward as he fell. His assailant flew over his head and sprawled among his companions.

Changa fell onto his back gasping for air. He threw the scarf aside and went for his weapons. The man in the green turban appeared over him, an evil grin on his face.

"You shall not have her," he hissed. "Even if you kill us more will come. She is Kali's daughter. She is our goddess. It does not matter if we do not kill you. If we don't, she will. It is her nature."

He disappeared. His cohorts attacked Changa with jagged knives raised over their heads, their eyes wide with fervor. Changa snatched up his sword and swung wide, cutting both men across their bellies. They collapsed in unison, their bodies falling atop their spilled entrails. Changa leaped over the dying men to Sharmila.

"Are you okay?" he asked.

Sharmila eyes blinked as she sat up. She touched her bruised face then glared at Changa. Her skin darkened and she shoved him away.

"Where is he?" she snarled.

Changa's eyes went wide. This was not the subservient woman he'd shared his bed with.

Changa stood. "He's gone."

Sharmila seemed to calm herself. "Is he dead?"

Changa shook his head. "No."

Sharmila sighed and slumped to her knees. Changa joined her.

"Who is this man? What is he to you?"

"I don't know his name," she answered. "He has haunted me since I was a child. He and his followers believe I am some incarnation of Kali."

Though he was not of this land, he was familiar with its people and its gods. He thought of her mesmerizing dance and the physical changes he witnessed.

"Are you?"

Sharmila snatched away from him. "No!"

Changa stood again. "I must go check on the camp. Will you be okay alone?"

Sharmila nodded without looking at him.

"Good." Changa left the tent. Men wandered about the damaged camp helping the wounded and gathering goods. The Thuggee were not after their goods; most of the cargo was unscathed except those trampled by the panicked elephants. Mikaili sauntered up to him, followed by a harried Ahmed.

"They didn't come to steal," Mikaili observed.

"They came for Sharmila," Changa answered.

Mikaili scratched his head. "She's a beautiful woman, but I don't think she's worth all this."

"They think she is some sort of goddess, a goddess named Kali."

"Kali?" Ahmed eyes widened.

Both Mikaili and Changa looked at Ahmed.

"What do you know of this Kali?" Changa asked him.

"She is the destroyer, the giver of life and the killer of demons," he replied. "The Thuggee worship her. They honor her by murder. But they do not usually attack in large numbers."

"Maybe it's time to tell her goodbye," Mikaili said. "We were lucky not to lose our cargo but now we don't have laborers to carry everything."

Changa rubbed his chin. "Ahmed, are there any villages nearby?"

"There is a small village a few miles south."

"We'll go there in the morning and see if we can hire more laborers. We'll leave the raja's tent. We don't have the manpower and I'll risk his wrath."

"And what of Sharmila?" Mikaili asked.

"She remains with us. We are almost to Goa. We will part

ways there."

Mikaili shook his head and walked away. Ahmed remained.

"Sahib, your friend may be right," he said.

"The Thuggee will not bother us again, at least not between here and Goa."

"You are probably right, sahib. But if this woman is who they think she is she is more dangerous than a thousand men."

"I will not leave Sharmila alone," Changa snapped. "We are done discussing this."

"Yes, sahib." Ahmed bowed and went about his business. Changa walked back to his tent. He couldn't deny Sharmila's strangeness, but he would not abandon her. There was no amount of wealth in the world worth the life of someone he cared for, and he did care for Sharmila. But if he did not return with his wealth, his chances to return home to free his mother and sisters would be greatly diminished.

Sharmila was dressed when he entered the tent. Her face was drawn.

"They wish for you to leave me," she said.

"Yes," Changa answered.

"I would not blame you if you did. I must be truthful. Many men have promised to protect me but all of them have failed. All of them have died. Yet you are the only one that has stood against the Thuggee and lived."

"I survived this time, but what about the next time? I am no god, I am just a man."

Sharmila came to him and wrapped her arms around her neck.

"No, you are more than just a man. The raja sensed it and I sense it, too."

She held him tighter and Changa responded, his arms circling her waist.

"When I was a child I once sought refuge in a Buddhist monastery. An elder monk told me of a place where I could be safe. He promised to take me there but never got the chance. The

Thuggee attacked and killed them all. I barely escaped."

This was something new, Changa thought.

"You know of this place?"

Sharmila turned away. "Not exactly. He spoke of an island where everyone lives in solitude and meditation. There is no violence or strife for the priests have the favor of all the gods and demons. If I were to go there I could finally be free of this life."

Changa rubbed his chin. "You will remain with us until we reach Goa. Once there we will find out about this island. If it exists Mikaili can find it. We will take you there."

Sharmila placed her head on his chest. "Thank you, Changa."

"Don't thank me yet," he answered. "We'll have to find this island first."

Sharmila looked into his eyes. "We will, Changa. Trust me."

6

THE RAJA'S REVENGE

Changa's caravan left Vijyanagar much larger than when it returned to Goa, but it was still impressive. Goans pointed and shouted as the line of men and elephants entered the city. Changa and Sharmila rode together as they had since leaving the capital city. Though his feelings were still strong for the mysterious woman, they were tainted by the Thuggee attack and Ahmed's revelations. Sharmila's arms tightened around his waist as if she sensed his doubts. He smiled; there was no need to worry. Whatever gifts she possessed would never be used against him. Of that he was certain.

They paraded through the city and the marketplace to the docks. Mikaili had taken the time to send a runner ahead so the baharia were waiting as they arrived. Zakee waved, his ever present smile the perfect greeting. The Tuareg stood beside him, a welcoming gleam in his eyes. Panya looked directly into Changa's eyes, a scowl on her face. There would be words between them once they were settled.

Changa's elephant knelt and he climbed down. He was helping Sharmila when Zakee arrived.

"You must tell me everything!" he shouted. "Is the City of Victory as beautiful as they claim?"

"Yes it is," Changa replied. His eyes strayed past Zakee to Panya. She busied herself with Ahmed, inspecting the merchandise while barking orders to the crew. It was not her duty but the men respected her words.

"Let's get everything aboard the dhows then I'll tell you anything you want," Changa finally replied. Zakee bowed and wandered in the chaos, his youthful curiosity rendering him totally useless.

Changa spied Mikaili and waved him over. The navigator took his time, occasionally swinging a disappointed look toward

Sharmila.

"Sharmila wishes us to take her to an island," he said.

"It is an island of priests," she said, her voice eager. "Changa says you are a well-traveled man and excellent navigator. Do you know of this island?"

"Changa lies," Mikaili spat. "I'll admit I've seen more of this world than most but I've never heard of your island of priests."

"So there is place that Mikaili cannot find," Changa smirked.

"I said I never heard of it," Mikaili retorted. "I didn't say I couldn't find it."

"Now how are you going to find something you never heard of?"

"I never heard of it," Mikaili admitted. "That doesn't mean someone in this city hasn't. There's at least one bahari here that knows about your holy island. The challenge is finding him."

"Then I suggest you get started," Changa urged. "The cargo will be loaded soon and we'll push off soon afterwards."

Mikaili's eyes widened. "Get started? I'm not…"

He glared at Changa and Sharmila.

"Come with me, woman," he growled. "Let's see if someone in this cesspool knows about your island. The sooner we find it and leave you on it the sooner my life gets back to normal."

Changa almost grinned until he considered Mikaili's words. They would leave Sharmila on the island if such a place existed. It was what she seemed to want but Changa wasn't sure it was what he wanted.

"She's still with you."

Panya stood behind him, her fists resting on her hips.

"If you have something to say, Panya, say it."

"I did but you wouldn't listen. Ahmed told me about the Thuggee attack."

"It was unexpected but we survived."

Panya rolled her eyes. "Can't you see what's happening? She controls you, Changa. These feeling you have for her are not true. She will keep you until she has no use for you."

"You're out of line," Changa snapped back. "What makes you think you can talk to me like this? I'm no village boy. I would know if I was being manipulated. Whatever feelings I have for Sharmila are mine. It is not your concern."

Panya glared at him, her body shaking visibly. "I only hope that when you come to your senses it won't be too late. This crew depends on your good judgment. They accept your word without question because they trust you."

"Then you should trust me as well," Changa replied.

Panya's eyes softened. "I can't. Not when you're like this."

Panya walked away. Changa thought of going after her then changed his mind. Panya had always given him good council, especially in matters of the spirits. Yet this time her words did not feel true to him. There was emotion behind him, whether anger or jealousy he did not know. He was beginning to think that their time in China was a bad idea.

The Tuareg saved him from his confusion. His hand touched Changa's shoulder then he pointed toward the market. A trio of elephants entered the throng from the north, lumbering slowly. Elephants in the market were not an unusual occurrence but these pachyderms were not carrying goods or supplies. These were war elephants, their tusks armed with steel blades and archers filled the carriages on their backs. The archers held loaded bows at their sides as they peered into the crowd.

"Damudar!" Changa exclaimed.

"Zakee!" Changa shouted. The young Yemeni ran up to his side.

"What is it, Changa?"

"Get the cargo loaded as soon as possible. Rally the Kazuri baharia with crossbows and swords."

Zakee's smile faded. He glanced toward the market and spotted the elephants.

"At once, Changa," he snapped.

"Come with me," Changa said to the Tuareg. They hurried

up to Ahmed and Panya.

"Ahmed, where would one go if they were seeking information on ports and islands?"

"There is a market section not far from my old shop. It is where the mapmakers work."

"Take us there. Panya, help Zakee get the dhows loaded. We may have to leave sooner than we planned."

Panya's stare spoke more than any words she could utter.

"We will not leave her," Changa answered.

Ahmed, Changa and the Tuareg hurried toward the market. The warriors were searching the central market and had yet to enter the side streets harboring the craftsmen. If they were lucky Mikaili and Sharmila would still be there. They were not lucky.

They heard the struggle before they saw it. People rushed past them, their excited voices a sign of what was ahead. Changa spied Mikaili and Sharmila pressed against a wall, Mikaili blocking Sharmila with his body. Five armed men formed a semi-circle before them, swords drawn. Two of them Changa recognized; they were Damudar's bodyguards. The armed men yelled at Mikaili in Hindi and Mikaili yelled back. Changa grinned; the old man was brave if nothing else.

Changa heaved a throwing knife and it buried into the head of the closest attacker. The others immediately attacked Changa and the Tuareg. Changa raised his sword to counter an overhead strike when a piercing scream overwhelmed him and he fell to the street.

"Leave me alone!"

Changa barely recognized Sharmila's voice. Tremors flashed under his body as he stood, blades drawn. Mikaili ran toward him with terror in his eyes.

"Come, Changa!" he shouted. "This is the devil's work!"

But Changa stood still, unable to move. Sharmila danced, not with the sultry cadence that enthralled him in the raja's tent but with stilted movements sharp and cruel. Her skin darkened as before but a bright iridescence outlined her frame, growing more intense with each step. She grew taller as well, twice as tall as

Changa. Then a bulge appeared on her side, gradually extending until it became an arm. She turned toward him, revealing another arm on the right side. Light matching the aura around her filled her eyes; she opened her hands and swords appeared, glowing like her aura.

Changa and the Tuareg backed away.

"Get back to the dhow as fast as you can," Changa said to his companion. "Tell Panya what you just saw."

The Tuareg gave Changa a questioning look. Changa snarled back.

"Go!" he yelled.

No sooner did the Tuareg turn to run did Sharmila leap toward them, her swords raised. Changa braced, rising to the balls of his feet while his knees bent. He had no idea what he was doing or what he was facing. Sharmila had transformed into something he had no knowledge of. Was she possessed by some malevolent spirit, or was this her true form? His mind went back to the conversation with the Thuggee. He'd called her Kali and said that she was to be worshipped. If this was what he sought, his death would not have been far behind. Changa was not sure if his life was any safer.

He jumped to the side as Sharmila's blades flashed down. Heat seared his check and he winced. Before he could stand completely the blades came at him again. It was a blistering attack, each blade seeking its own path with blinding speed. Changa twisted like an acrobat as he met fiery blades with Kongo iron. His arms quaked with every blow blocked and the ground under his feet shuddered with every step in Sharmila's martial dance. Though her blades wreaked destruction on the surrounding buildings Changa's knives held firm. He held the knives of the Kabaka, metal weapons forged by royal blacksmiths and imbued with the mysterious powers of his lineage. Whatever strength they possessed matched the power of Sharmila's swords. Changa was another matter. Though his strength and skills far surpassed that of a normal man, he was still of flesh and blood. His breath came harder with each moment passed; his muscled ached with each stroke deflected. He looked into Sharmila's eyes searching for any hint of recognition but her blazing orbs gave no mercy. If her derisive smile was to be believed, she would not stop until her mystic swords cleaved Changa's flesh.

Changa braced himself for another assault when a powerful gust of wind consumed him. Sharmila suddenly rose into the air and crashed into the building to the right. She stood immediately and was struck again. She diminished, the extra arms absorbed back into her body, her skin lightening to her golden brown complexion. She lay on the stone street naked, curled like a sleeping child.

Changa smiled with relief. The Tuareg and Panya galloped up to him astride horses with the Tuareg holding the reins of a third. Changa sprinted to the horse and jumped into the saddle.

"Thank you, Panya," he said with a relieved smile on his face. Panya did not return his joy.

"We must leave now," she warned. "Oya is stronger here than the Middle Kingdom but not strong enough."

"We will not leave her," Changa said. The Tuareg eyes widened and Panya's mouth dropped open.

"She has driven you mad!" Panya shouted. "You see her as she truly is and still you protect her. Can't you see she doesn't need you? She will kill you as surely as she killed the raja's men."

"We will not leave her," Changa reiterated. "This is not Sharmila. Something possesses her which she cannot control. Maybe the priests of this island of which she speaks can help her."

Changa rode up to Sharmila and dismounted. He waved Panya and the Tuareg to him and they reluctantly joined him.

"Do you have your sleeping powder?" Changa asked Panya.

Panya rustled through her pouch and took out a blue bag. "Yes I do."

"Give it to her. We can get her to the ship and set sail before the raja's men regroup."

"Changa, why are you so persistent about her? Can't you see she is a danger to us all?"

"I see a woman who is trapped by something she cannot

control. I'm not certain if my feelings are my own or if they come from her demands. What I do know is that either she will die or others will if we leave her here."

Panya's gaze softened. "I'm sure the words you spoke are yours, Changa."

Panya dipped her fingers in the bag then placed them on Sharmila's lips. Sharmila licked instinctively then sighed as the powder took effect. Changa lifted her onto his horse and the three galloped through the panicked crowd to their waiting ships.

"Let's get under way!" Changa shouted. The baharia worked quickly to load the remainder of the cargo then shoved away in good time. The raja's men and regrouped and made their way to the shore. A few managed to fire a few arrows at the fleeing fleet but they landed harmlessly in the surf. Changa carried Sharmila below deck and placed her gently into his bunk. He closed and locked his cabin door then smiled at the futility of the gesture. If she transformed into the thing he fought in Goa there would be no saving his dhow. He was playing with the life of his crew by bringing her aboard, but his instinct told him this was the right thing to do. He went to the deck and to Mikaili.

"How long will it take us to reach this island?"

"A week if the winds hold," he replied. The old navigator looked at Changa intensely.

"Do you love this woman?"

"No," Changa replied. "What feelings that grew between us were probably not true. But I will not abandon someone in need. Let's hope she will find the peace she seeks on this island."

"And what if this island does not hold what she seeks?"

Changa did not answer, for he did not have one.

***

A warm bright sun hovered in a clear blue sky, sharing its light on the small lush island below. The oval spot of land was tiny compared to its brethren that loomed in the distance, its width and breadth barely a day's walk. A thin strip of sand surrounded the thick jungle that made the interior. The island's elevation rose sharply before ending with a jagged peak of stone. Cut from the stone was a formidable stepped building similar to the temples of Vijayanagar although decorated less richly as their distant counterparts. Changa, Panya, and Zakee occupied the narrow beach with Sharmila lying on a coarse blanket still under the sway of Panya's somnolent concoction. They watched the narrow trail that pierced the foliage, the trail that Mikaili and the Tuareg took hours ago to the temple.

"What's taking them so long?" Changa groused.

"The wonders of the island are unknown to us," Zakee answered. "They may have encountered many amazing distractions along the way."

"Or dangerous ones," Panya added.

"Mikaili is not a man to be distracted by frivolous sights," Changa retorted. "Nor is the Tuareg. And I doubt if there is anything as dangerous on this speck as the Tuareg."

Mikaili and the Tuareg emerged from the jungle as if summoned. Three bald men dressed in orange robes draped over their right shoulders followed them. When the men spied Sharmila they scurried by the two and rushed up to her, their excited eyes darting between Changa and the woman. One of the priests began talking swiftly, wiggling his head from side to side with his companions.

Mikaili began to translate as he reached them.

"They are grateful that we have brought her to them. She has been expected for some time."

Changa was reminded of the Thuggee and reached into his knife bag.

"No, Changa. I know what you're thinking. These priests are not like the Thuggee. They won't worship her and they won't murder innocent people in her honor. Sharmila was right to come here."

"So what is their purpose?"

Mikaili talked to the priest and he quickly answered.

"The world is a place of strangeness and wonder. Sometimes,

even though they are above us, the gods meddle in our lives. Sometimes when a child is created he or she catches the interest of a particular god. This god will touch the child in its mother's womb, passing on a portion of its essence to the child. That child is born into a world that either worships or abuses them."

"So what does this have to do with Sharmila?"

"These priests established their temple to help such as her. Sharmila was touched by Kali, one of the most powerful of all gods. Her path is the hardest for she usually kills those who try to help her."

The priests looked at Changa with an expression bordering on admiration.

"Well, she's here now. Panya, revive her."

Panya extracted a green power from one of her pouches and touched Sharmila's lips. The god-child's eyelids fluttered immediately and she squinted as she adjusted to the bright sunlight.

"Changa?" she inquired.

"I am here, Sharmila, and we are on your island."

Sharmila sat up immediately and gazed into the peaceful faces of the priests. She smiled and her eyes glistened. Before Changa could speak again Sharmila wrapped her arms around him and kissed him deeply.

"I knew you were the one," she whispered. "This is where I belong, where I can live in peace."

She pulled away from him. "Stay with me."

Changa held her face between his hands. "I can't. This is not my path. I promised to bring you here and I have. The priests will take care of you far beyond what I can do. It's time I got back to my own life."

Sharmila's eyes drifted to Panya.

"Let him into your life," she said. "Changa is a man of no shadows. You know this, sister."

With that she stood and bowed to the priests. In an afterthought she ran to Changa and reached into his knife bag and pulled out a knife.

"A keepsake," she explained. She took off one of her bracelets and put it in his bag.

"So you will remember me. Goodbye, Changa Diop."

Sharmila and the priests disappeared into the jungle. Changa's smile faded as they disappeared from view. Sharmila was safe. It was time he got on with his work. He glanced at Panya as he dropped his arm around Zakee's shoulders.

"How far are we from Aden?" he asked.

Zakee's eyes brightened. "A few weeks at the most."

"Good, it's about time I fulfilled another promise. It's time I took you home."

KITABU CHA TANO:
(BOOK FIVE)
THE AMIR RETURNS

1

HOMECOMING

The bow of the *Kazuri* cut through the mild ocean waters, white foam splattering her hull. A persistent wind filled her sails as her deck swarmed with baharia absorbed in their daily chores. A dhow was a living thing in constant need of care. There were few moments for rest, which made the solitary figure motionless on the bow stand out among the activity.

Zakee was going home. Changa observed his young friend gazing into the horizon, a wide smile on his face. He thought back to the day they found him filthy and wounded in the forest, the jade obelisk clutched in his bleeding hands. Back then his only impression of the young amir was an unwelcomed distraction and a possible ransom for his return. So much time had passed since then. Zakee had become a member of his crew, a sometimes annoying member, but a member nonetheless. His training as a future sheik helped them immensely and he'd grown into a fine swordsman under the Tuareg's tutelage. Still, it was hard to see him as a grown man.

Changa abandoned the wheel and walked to Zakee's side. The young man jumped, a worried look on his face. The shocked look transformed to a smile.

"Always be aware of your surroundings," Changa chided. "I thought I taught you that."

"I'm on the Kazuri, the safest dhow on the sea," Zakee replied. "If I cannot drop my guard here then I am in hell."

The two shared a brief laughed before Zakee's face took on a solemn tone.

"I have so much on my mind," he said. "I knew that one day I would return to Aden. Now that that day is near my heart is filled with confusion."

"What is there to be confused about? You're going home. Your family will be joyous to see you and I will be rewarded for returning you alive and sound."

Zakee struggled to smile. "You have been like an uncle to me and the Tuareg like a brother. My father taught me many things of Yemen, but you taught me about the world."

Changa shrugged. "I taught you nothing. I just needed an extra hand to mend the sails."

Zakee broke into one of his boisterous laughs. "You always downplay, but I know you understand."

"So why are you confused?"

"What will my parents think when I return? They probably think I am dead."

"They probably think you are a happily married man too busy to visit them which would be understandable if you were a sheik."

Zakee nodded knowingly. "You speak of Bahati. It has been a long time since I thought of her. The last time my parents saw me I was sailing off as a happy husband. Much has happened since then."

"Don't worry, Zakee," Changa said and he laid his hand on Zakee's shoulder. "Aden is your city, is it not?"

Zakee was smiling again. "Yes, she is my city."

"So we will be showered with gifts and songs will be sung in our honor."

"I hope so, Changa. I truly hope so."

Aden revealed her proximity long before she came into view as Changa's fleet became a few dhows among many. Like other ports of her status Aden was a busy and wealthy city, an important rest stop and transfer point for goods destined for the Swahili Coast and points beyond. Zakee's nervousness increased with every league sailed; he paced the deck and wrung his hands.

"You'd think he was awaiting a bride," Mikaili commented.

"He's going home," Panya chimed in. "He should be nervous."

"I would think he'd be happy."

Panya looked at Changa and rolled her eyes. At least she

was responding to him now. There was still some distance between them but the conversation was reassuring.

"Zakee was his father's favorite when he left. I'm sure that status has changed. One of his brothers may be first in line now, and we know how ambition can cut the ropes of fraternity."

Changa nodded. "He has a place with us."

They joined the parade of vessels sailing for the harbor. Aden hugged the coast, occupying a thin strip of beach at the base of a group of imposing peaks. One and two story stone buildings surrounded the harbor then climbed onto the hillsides, almost reaching the summits themselves. Minarets rose above the mundane structures. As they came closer the city mosque could be seen in close proximity to a striking multilevel building that towered over the city like an ancient cedar tree.

Zakee pointed to the building. "My home!" He grasped the Tuareg's arm and shook it like a child asking for a treat.

"You will love it! Aden is one of the richest cities of my land, second only to Sana'a. All of you will be treated with honor." Changa and the Tuareg looked skeptically at each other.

"One thing at a time, Zakee," Changa said. "Let's make sure your return is welcomed."

Zakee looked at Changa with a puzzled look on his face.

"We'll take the Kazuri in," Changa said. "The Hazina and Sendibada will stay in deep water."

Mikaili pulled at his beard. "Are you expecting trouble?"

"I'm not expecting anything," Changa replied. "Just being prepared." He looked at his young friend. "Are you ready?"

Zakee took on a regal pose. "Yes, Changa, I am."

Changa grinned. "Then let's take you home."

The *Kazuri* cruised in close along a clear spot of beach. Changa, Zakee, and the Tuareg disembarked at the bow into a transport boat and rowed to shore. No sooner did their feet touch sand did a man with a high turban and a ragged beard approach them with tablet and quill in hand.

"What is your purpose here?" he said.

"I am Amir Zakee ibn Basheer," Zakee announced.

The man frowned at Zakee as he squinted.

"Be careful what you say," he spat. "Amir Zakee was an honored man. His death was mourned for three months. You and your Zanj servants best be gone before the authorities get wind of your attempt at deception."

"Maybe this will convince you." Zakee opened his robe, revealing an object that Changa did not know the young prince possessed. A dagger with an angled sheath pressed against his belly, a jeweled handle extending over the waist belt. The man's eyes widened as his mouth dropped open.

"I wonder where he kept that hidden?" Changa whispered to the Tuareg. The Tuareg shrugged.

The man fell to his knees. "Allah is great! Amir Zakee has returned!"

He jumped to his feet then ran about, shouting as loud as he could.

"Amir Zakee has returned! Zakee is here!"

Others looked in their direction. Zakee placed his hands on his hips, his jeweled jambiya clearly visible. A crowd gathered around them filled with astonished and bewildered faces.

"Baharia! Come keep our brother company!" Changa shouted.

Changa and the Tuareg did the best they could keeping the crowd back while the baharia emptied the *Kazuri*. When they finally reached the shore they quickly formed a protective perimeter around Zakee, Changa, and the Tuareg.

"We should go to the palace," Zakee said.

"No, we wait here," Changa advised. "If this turns bad we have the Kazuri behind us and our other dhows not far away."

"But look at them!" Zakee said. "They know who I am!"

The Tuareg placed his hand on Zakee's shoulder. His eyes were concerned and solemn.

"I understand, my brother. I will be patient." He nodded to Changa. "Forgive me, Changa. Your advice is always well founded."

Changa noticed the suspicious looks that fell upon him.

"I think it would be wise that we defer to you for the time being," Changa said. "Your Yemeni don't seem to take kindly to a Zanj giving their amir orders or advice."

"As you say," Zakee agreed. "Once we are at the palace I will explain everything to them."

Commotion and movement in the distance caught Changa's eye. Horsemen wearing conical helmets and brandishing lances made a path through the gathering throng.

"Now it begins," Changa mused.

The horsemen spread out before the baharia, their lances lowered. They parted in the center of their line and a horseman cloaked in silks and a white turban rode forward. He dismounted and stormed toward the baharia, his round goateed face locked in a stern expression.

"What is this?" he bellowed. "Are you the ones who have… Amir Zakee?"

"Asif Ahmad!" Zakee exclaimed.

Changa nodded then the baharia stepped aside. The two men rushed then hugged.

"I do not believe my eyes! What have I done that Allah has allowed me to see this day?"

The horsemen lowered their lances, their stern expressions replaced by smiles.

"It is true!" someone shouted. "It is Zakee!"

Zakee patted Asif's back. "I have much to tell you, and I'm sure you have much to tell, but first I must visit my mother and father."

Asif's countenance dulled. "Amir, much as changed since you've been gone. Most of it not for the better."

"What are you saying?" Zakee's face paled.

"Your father is dead," Asif revealed.

Changa placed a comforting hand on Zakee's shoulder. He knew well the pain of the loss of a father. At least Zakee wasn't a witness to a death as gruesome as Changa's father.

Zakee closed his eyes and lowered his head. When he looked up his expression was solemn.

"How did he die?"

"As I said, Amir, much has changed. Yemen is threatened by forces beyond our imagination."

Zakee looked at Changa and the Bakonga frowned. Their journey seemed destined for strange adventures and it seemed another was about to begin.

"Let us go to the palace," Zakee said.

"Will your servants accompany us?"

Zakee grinned. "These are not my servants. They are my companions. As a matter of fact while on the seas I answer to this man. He is Changa Diop."

Asif smiled and bowed. "So you are the great Changa Diop!"

Changa chuckled. "It seems my name follows the clouds."

"This is a port city and a busy one at that. Anyone who has caused grief for the Sangir is well known and well loved. You chose the right man to be lost with, Amir."

Zakee managed to smile. "That I did."

Asif ordered two of his guardsmen to dismount and offered the horses to Changa and the Tuareg. They rode though the crowded *souk,* the people bowing and shouting salutations to their returning amir. The procession followed the narrow roads upward to the city center and the palace. Zakee's home was a series of buildings built about an outcrop that rose in the city center. The palace cast a shadow on the mosque below, a fact that seemed planned. They pushed through the crowd and into the formal courtyard, a lavish garden centered on a rectangular pond. Zakee was barely off his horse before six women rushed through the doors opposite the gate, their ululations rising over the street din. Zakee ran to them and was engulfed in hugs, tears, and kisses.

Changa and the Tuareg strolled up to the emotional reunion.

"You did not tell us you had other wives, Zakee," Changa commented.

Zakee extracted himself from the affectionate hands. "No, Changa, these are not my wives. These are my sisters."

Zakee began shifting and arranging his sisters as they chatted away in Arabic, pointed at each one as he said their names.

"This is Asmaa, Baseerah, Tasheem, Jameelah, Kahdeejah and Zharaa."

He looked at Kahdeejah, the tallest of the group whose eyes flickered from joy to worry.

"Why are you here?" he asked. "You should be in Sana'a."

"Sana'a has become too dangerous," she replied in a sweet voice. "The Red Sheikh's arm comes closer every day. Wazeer sent us here for our protection."

"Wazeer? Did father choose him as sultan?"

"You were his choice."

Changa lifted his head as another woman entered the room, a woman whose age and dignity reflected in her gait. Zakee left his sisters immediately and went to the woman. They hugged and cried as his sisters joined them.

"Zakee, Allah has answered my prayers."

"I am home, mamma."

Zakee's mother looked at Changa and the Tuareg and nodded.

"I am Zaleekhah. Thank you for taking care of my son. He was safer in your hands than if he had remained here."

"I'm not so sure about that," Changa commented. "But he is here alive. I guess that says something."

"Come inside everyone," Asif insisted. "There is much we must discuss."

Asif led them to a sitting room. An expansive rug covered the marble floor; a low table occupied the center of the room surrounded by ornate chairs that resembled small thrones. Zakee's sisters took their turns kissing his cheeks then left the room. Asif and Zahleekhah sat first; Zakee sat near his mother and Changa and the Tuareg sat opposite them.

"Two years after your disappearance rumors swirled from the desert of a clan chief attempting to unite the nomads under the old ways," Asif explained. "Your father showed little concern. As you know the nomads have always been a nuisance and occasionally a threat. It was his opinion to let them form their nation. It would be easier to crush with them in one place than to roam the desert looking for them."

Changa nodded; it seemed a good strategy to him.

Asif sighed as he rubbed his forehead. "Two years later the rumors were proven true. The clan chief called himself the Red Sultan. He claimed all of Yemen as his land. He was so bold as to send a message to your father declaring his intentions. He offered to let him live if he gave up his seat peacefully."

"It was the emissary that first revealed this Red Sheikh was no ordinary man," his mother said. "He arrived on a camel draped in rich fabrics and jewels. A red *shemagh* covered his face except his eyes, which were eerie in that the man did not blink. He rode to the palace and demanded a meeting with your father which was of course refused."

"It was good that he did," Asif continued. "For then the messenger removed his scarf and revealed a face of death. His skin was pale like that of the dead and his stench sickened the guards. He announced his demand with a voice too loud for a normal man then stood motionless as he awaited an answer. Your father appeared in his balcony and refused the messenger's demands. No sooner did the refusal leave his lips did the messenger collapse where he stood. A greenish gas escaped from his orifices, killing the guards surrounding him. There was a panic that was quelled by persistent calls from the imams for order and prayers."

They sat silent for a moment. Asif's words sent a chill through Changa; the images of the tebos intruding on his calm. He exchanged knowing glances with the Tuareg and Zakee. This was a story familiar to them.

"The threat was obvious," Asif continued, his voice subdued. "Basheer declared jihad against the Red Sheikh and raised an army to march against him. He took your brothers and ten thousand faithful warriors into the sands to face the infidel. He did not return. Only one hundred men survived, your brothers among them."

Zakee looked stunned, his mouth open. "Where are my

brothers?"

"They are in Sana'a. They have closed the gates to the city and prepare for siege," his mother spat. "They will not speak of the battle, nor will they raise another army to avenge Basheer's death."

"Maybe the Red Sheikh is more powerful that you imagined," Changa suggested. "A defensive strategy may be more prudent."

"They are afraid!" Zahleekhah shouted. "They send us away to protect us then squabble over the throne as the Red Sheikh marches to the mountains with his horde."

"It seems that your return is fortuitous," Changa commented.

Zakee's stunned look remained. "What are you saying?"

"It is well known that you were your father's favorite," his mother said. "It broke his heart when you left with Bahati. Allah has seen to your return so you can take your place and avenge your father's death."

Khadeejah, his oldest sister, entered the room as if summoned. She carried an ebony box trimmed in gold metal and jewels. She knelt beside Zakee and placed the box before him.

"Open it," his mother commanded.

Zakee lifted the lid and gasped. He reached into the box and extracted a jeweled sheath, the end bent at a sharp angle. A hilt of kifaru horn studded with gold, emeralds, and diamonds protruded from the sheath.

"It is your father's jambiya, the family heirloom," his mother confirmed. "Neither Wazeer or Khaalid can claim the throne without it. Will you accept your destiny, Zakee?"

Zakee removed the knife from the sheath and held it before him. He looked at Changa.

"It's your decision," he said.

"I must avenge my father and deal with this Red Sheikh. Will you help me?"

"You are part of my crew. Do you need to ask?"

Zakee flashed his familiar grin. "Then I accept my destiny. I will go to Sana'a."

Amir jumped to his feet and bowed deeply "Sultan Zakee! What is your command?"

Despite his acceptance of his title Zakee looked stunned. He stared at his mother's approving eyes then turned to Changa and the Tuareg.

"What do I do?" he asked.

Changa hesitated before he replied. He loathed the task of advisor although he often found himself doing as much. First Mulefu, then Tumen Khan, now a man that he looked at as a little brother. Everyone in the room looked at him expectantly except the Tuareg. His silent companion's demeanor reflected his evaluating attitude.

"To accept the sultanate is to declare war on the Red Sheikh…and your brothers," he finally said. Zakee's eyes widened and his mouth dropped open.

"You must raise an army then march to Sana'a. Settle the dispute between your brothers then deal with the sheikh. You will need Panya's help with the latter."

"My brothers? Why must I fight them?"

"He speaks the truth," Asif said. "They will not accept your role peacefully. Wazeer certainly won't. Khaalid may be more reasonable. Either way, you need to be prepared to fight."

"I'm sad to say these words are true," his mother agreed. "Wazeer has practically claimed the sultanate by his actions. He and his men control Sana'a. Khaalid's forces equal Wazeer's but most remain outside the citadel. He has been agreeable to Wazeer's commands because Wazeer is the elder."

Zakee rubbed his chin, a gesture adopted from Changa. "It seems Khaalid may be more willing to follow than lead."

Changa and the Tuareg passed knowing glances. "Khaalid plays his own game, I think. You must be careful with both."

Zakee sighed. "This will be very difficult. We were not close because of our circumstances but they are my brothers."

"You must clear your head of whatever fraternal feelings you have of them," Changa urged. "They are your rivals. They will either rule you or be ruled by you. That is the truth of your situation."

"So it is decided on what I should do," Zakee confirmed. "Now how do I do it? If the Red Sheikh is on the march then time is of the essence. How long will it take to raise an army?"

Again Asif spoke. "The army is ready. I have acted as regent of Aden since you departed. When we received the word of your father's defeat and your brothers' retreat to Sana'a I requested a force to augment the garrison to protect the port. I was refused. Assuming we were on our own I took it on myself to increase the size of the garrison and reinforce the north walls."

Changa grinned as he nodded. Asif was a smart man.

"How many soldiers do we have?"

"Five thousand full time, another four thousand in the militia. We also have a force of two thousand Turkomen mercenaries in reserve."

The word mercenary made Changa frown. Zakee noticed and repeated his gesture. Asif noticed both of their gestures and his eyes widened.

"The Turkomen are not ordinary mercenaries, Sultan. They are loyal to their employer and braver than most soldiers. Besides they are aware that the Red Sheikh is an infidel. They will serve well if they are needed."

"That remains to be seen," Changa commented.

Asif nodded respectfully. "I understand your concerns, Changa. I have an additional reason to trust them. They are my countrymen."

Changa smiled as he considered this new bit of information. Asif had a force loyal to him as well.

"We will not solve this dilemma today," Changa said. "For now I would like to get my people settled and I know you have much to share with your family, Zakee."

Zakee's boyish grin returned. "Yes I do, Changa."

"The Tuareg and I will return to the dhows. We might as well do some trading while we're here. We'll discuss the situation with everyone and see what we can do to help."

Asif stood with them. "I'll have an escort take you to the landings."

Changa patted Zakee's shoulder.

"Not quite the homecoming you expected."

Zakee repeated the gesture. "I am home, Changa. That means more than anything else."

Changa and the Tuareg walked through the palace, Asif close behind. When they stepped out Asif's men waited for them with three extra horses. Two of the horses were saddled; the other possessed a large canvas bag on its back.

"We are grateful for Zakee's return," Asif said. "It is obvious you treated him well during your journeys and he has great respect for you both. Now that he is home he no longer has use of you."

Changa smirked. "I'll admit when I found Zakee running ragged through the forest my intentions were to return him home for a handsome payment. But since that time he has become a trusted member of my crew. Your ransom, though generous, is not necessary. Zakee needs someone he can trust. So far I don't see anyone that he can. Besides, Sultan Zakee has asked me to be his councilor."

Asif's eyes narrowed. "I served the amir faithfully during his rule of Aden. When he disappeared with Bahati no one mourned more than I. I administered this city in hopes that I would have the privilege of relinquishing control to Sultan Zakee and take my rightful place as his servant."

"Yet you raised an army and hired two thousands of your own countrymen to 'protect' the richest city in Yemen." Changa rubbed his chin. "Such loyalty is admirable."

Both men studied each other. The Tuareg kept his eyes on Asif's men; his skilled hands close to the hilts of his swords.

"So you refuse the ransom for service to the sultan?" Asif asked.

"We refuse the payment, but we will not refuse Zakee. He is our companion and we will advise and protect him the best we can."

Asif released a wide smile. "I believe you, Changa. A

selfish man would have taken the ransom without hesitation."

"I'm happy you're satisfied although your opinion means nothing to me."

Asif's smile diminished. "Oh, it should. If you had taken the ransom you and your dhows would rest at the bottom of our harbor."

"You would find that extremely difficult to accomplish," Changa answered.

Asif nodded. "Probably so, but I would try."

They had reached an understanding. Although Changa still didn't trust Asif completely he was convinced that the regent had the young amir's best interest in mind. It seemed that the man had come to the same conclusion about him.

"We'll return to our dhows and brief our crew," Changa explained. "It seems we'll be staying longer than we expected."

When they returned to their dhows Mikaili and Panya were waiting. Mikaili stared at them both impatiently while Panya's concern revealed she knew more than she should.

"It seems that our friend Zakee is the Sultan of Yemen," Changa announced.

Mikaili rolled his eyes. "Why can't we have a normal port call?"

Panya pushed by the recalcitrant navigator and stood before Changa, looking at him directly for the first time in months.

"What else?" she asked.

"It seems the sultanate is at war with a usurper called the Red Sheikh."

Panya nodded her head as if his words confirmed her thoughts.

Changa continued. "He killed Zakee's father and most of his brothers. The two brothers that remain control Sana'a, the capital city. Zakee's mother offered him the sultanate and he accepted. He plans to take an army to Sana'a, claim the sultanate and fight the Red Sheikh. We're going to help him."

Mikaili threw up his hands and stalked away. Panya remained before him.

"Is there more?"

"It seems our Red Sheikh is either a man of skills or has people of power serving him. He sent a corpse with a message of surrender to Zakee's father and when the sultan refused the corpse released a gas that killed many."

Panya nodded slowly. "Then we will help him."

"Your skills will be very important I think," Changa noted.

A smile came to her face. "They always are with you."

"This is for Zakee, not for me."

"The spirits follow you. You should know this by now. They forge your spirit like a blade."

Darkness crept through Changa as the image of tebos appeared in his mind. Usenge's servants seem to always find him, even in the far reaches of the Mongol grasslands.

"The Red Sheikh is not my challenge; he is Zakee's. We will make sure our brother is safe before we set sail."

"Of course. I will consult with those of my kind and see what I can learn."

"I doubt if you learn much," Changa replied. "The Yemeni seem to be fervent Muslims."

Panya smiled. "The old ways always linger."

"First things first. We have to secure the dhows. We'll share the news with the crew and let them make their choices."

"They'll agree to stay," Panya answered. "Especially the Kazuri baharia. They consider Zakee one of their own."

"Still we must ask. It is our way."

The baharia gathered on the *Hazina*, Changa's largest dhow. Changa stood by the center mast as his men surrounded him, their faces expectant. This was not the first time they'd had such a meeting during this safari and each meeting resulted in a unique and dangerous adventure. But in those cases he had asked them to follow him into a dangerous endeavor. They had done so knowing that success meant generous payment. This was different.

"My brothers! Once again I come to you with a proposal. Hear me with both ears and think on my words before you answer.

We've come a long way from Sofala and we've done some things that make the words of the greatest storyteller seem like sand on a beach. Each of you possesses enough goods to make you rich enough to buy your own dhows. I hope not, because I couldn't survive the competition!"

A joyful laugh rippled through the throng. Changa's smile faded as he prepared to deliver his next words.

"Zakee has been among us for many months now and he has become one of our crew. Today I witnessed something I never expected to see. Our companion has become sultan of Yemen." Changa let the murmur subside before he continued. "Now I know what some of you are thinking but get it out of your head. There will be no ransom."

A collective groan rose from the combined crews and Changa shook his head. Greed ends only when it's buried, the saying went.

"Zakee's new status comes with a price. He gained the title at the expense of his father's death. Yemen is at war. As we speak a man who calls himself the Red Sheikh leads his army against Sana'a, Yemen's capital city. Zakee must raise an army to protect the city and proclaim his leadership among his people. He needs our help."

Changa was disappointed by the grumbling he heard from everyone except the *Kazuri* baharia. They sat up straight, their faces serious. Like Panya said earlier, Zakee was their brother. They were ready to do whatever he asked.

"We are too few to make much difference to Zakee's war plans, but we are numerous enough to stand by our companion and make sure no harm comes to him during this dangerous time. He needs our council, our protection, and our support."

Changa remained silent to let his words soak in. The *Kazuri* sailors were still attentive. The others seemed to contemplate his words.

"As always it is your choice. Those who can handle a sword will be needed. The others will stay here with the dhows and be prepared to do whatever is needed. If you wish to take your earnings and return to Sofala I will arrange safe transport for you. Whatever you decide to do you will remain my brothers."

Changa stepped down from the mast and walked through his men. The *Kazuri* baharia surrounded him immediately led by Maliki, the *nahoda* of the *Kazuri*.

"What must we do?" he asked.

"Accompany me to the palace," Changa replied. "I need half the crew to remain with the dhow just in case we need the Kazuri's special skills. You decide among yourselves who will come. I have to tell you all this will be a very dangerous safari. I believe Zakee is in great danger. I also believe he can trust no one but us."

Maliki nodded. "We'll get our weapons."

Changa watched them leave the *Hazina* then went to his cabin. The others would be more discreet to avoid any hostility from the others if they decided not to join the others.

Changa sat patiently as baharia came to his cabin one by one, each signing on to the new adventure. Most were sincere, some were hedging their bets on an eventual payoff, and a few were responding to the silent pressure of their comrades. The last to come to his tent was Mikaili. He stood before Changa, worrying the Coptic cross dangling from a gold chain around his neck. He was frowning as always.

"So our pup is a wolf in his homeland," he finally said.

"No, he's still a pup," Changa replied. "He's being forced into a role he's not ready for."

"Succession usually happens this way. He'll learn or he'll die."

Changa couldn't hide his shock. Mikaili was usually acerbic but this was too far even for him.

"Say what you've come to say," Changa insisted.

"This is foolish!" Mikaili ranted. "The boy should get back on this dhow and leave with us. Let his brothers deal with this Red Sheikh."

"His mother says he was chosen before he left with Bahati," Changa replied. "She gave him his father's jambiya. Once he accepted it he set his course."

Mikaili's head jerked away and Changa realized what he was witnessing. The old navigator was worried about Zakee! Mikaili finally turned to look at Changa. "I'm an old man. I should be in the mountains of my homeland scolding my grandchildren and watching goats. My arm is too weak to wield a sword well and my legs are too sore to take on a campaign. But I can sail a dhow to the edge of the sea if need be and I can outsmart the craftiest pirate alive."

"So you're with us?"

Mikaili's face shriveled as if he'd smelled something bad. "Of course I am!"

"Good." Changa stood. "I must return to the palace. Keep an eye on these sea rats. Try to work in some trading while we're here as well. We might as well take advantage of the opportunity."

"Always thinking of profit," Mikaili chided.

Changa smiled. "Always."

Changa gathered with the *Kazuri* baharia at the beach. One more person was missing. She finally appeared, draped in talismans and a host of gourds hanging from her shoulders.

"I see you found some useful items," Changa said.

Panya beamed. "The medicines here are very familiar. Some are from Swahililand and a few are from my home."

"I'm impressed."

Panya's face took on a somber expression. "What I found is not as important as what I heard."

"What do you mean?"

"The Red Sheikh is closer than anyone realizes. His army may rest at the foothills but his magic is already at work in Aden. Healers struggle to treat the sick as their potions lose their potency. Diviners find their predictions obscured by a veil of uncertainty. There is even talk of the dead rising from their graves and marching off into the desert."

"You believe this?"

Panya nodded. "Not all, but some may be true. I feel this land is off balance somehow and what my brethren tell me seems to fit my concerns. We will have to make sure Zakee is protected."

"He won't accept any of your trinkets. You know this."

"He doesn't have to wear them as long as they are near."

"We can probably manage that."

Changa looked up into the hazy sky.

"Come, we've been gone too long. We have a sultan to protect."

Changa and the others gathered before the dhows. They were met by the garrison horsemen and escorted to the palace.

Crowds of Yemenis ogled the Sofalans and their escort as they made their way to Aden's palace. The palace guards opened the gates despite the suspicious looks on their faces. The Sofalans paid no attention to the scrutiny. They had been in the position many times. Zakee, his family, and his growing entourage met them in the courtyard. The new sultan smiled warmly.

"I was happy to be with my family again, but I'm most happy to be among my brothers!"

He worked his way through the *Kazuri* baharia, hugging and speaking with each man before turning his attention to Changa and Panya.

"I did not know you would be coming too, Lady Panya," he said graciously. "You must meet my mother and sisters."

Zakee towed Panya to the women before she had a chance to protest. Changa followed, amused at Zakee's exuberance. The weight of the sultanate had yet to settle on his mind.

The Basheer women did not seem happy with Panya. Their faces formed a wall of displeasure as Zakee introduced her.

"Mother, this is Panya. She is the priestess and healer for our crew. Her talents are as incredible as her beauty."

"I would think you would have had your fill of Zanj women," his mother remarked.

Zakee's eyes went wide then he laughed. "No, mother. Panya is not my wife. She is bonded to Changa."

Panya glanced back at Changa as if looking for some confirmation. Changa stiffened and his mouth formed a tight line. The tension between them had waned but they had yet to sit down and discuss anything. So if Panya was expecting some sort of clarification before Zakee and his family she was not going to get it.

"I claim no man among these men and no man claims me," she said as she bowed slightly. "I know you consider my presence among them unveiled and not chaperoned questionable but I assure you I am not what you think. The Sofalans treat me as a sister." She glanced at Changa again but the surly Bakonga said nothing.

"I have always trusted Zakee's judgment, even when it was not the best," his mother finally said. "His praise is usually high but deserved. I welcome you, Panya."

"Enough pleasantries," Changa growled. "There's a war on and we must win it. Panya, tell everyone what you have discovered."

"The Red Sheikh may rest beyond the mountains but his influence seeps into the streets of Aden. His powers affect the soothsayers and conjurers and his nearness weakens the healers' potions."

"They are infidels!" Asif exclaimed. "Their skills were never true. This is not indication of the Red Sheikh."

Panya shrugged. "Believe what you wish. I respect your god and your faith. I can only tell you what I see, feel, and hear. Zakee is familiar with my talents. He will decide whether to heed my words."

Zakee looked briefly at Asif then faced Panya. "So what does this mean?"

"If the sheikh is having such an influence on Aden imagine what havoc he wreaks in Sana'a." Panya looked at everyone. "The sooner we go to Sana'a the better."

Asif moved close to Zakee. "My sultan! I have been your friend and companion long before these Zanj took you captive. I see where their influence comes now. It is her, the witch. Surely you have not forgotten Bahati so quickly. I warned you about her and now I warn you again."

"I have always trusted your word and council Asif, but this time you are wrong." Zakee stood between Changa and Panya. "I have traveled to places I never dreamed existed and experienced adventures that would astound the imams. All the while my friends have kept me safe. Panya's ways are those of the infidel, but her potions and powers have saved us from many dangers, combined with my prayers to Allah, of course. Changa's mind is as sharp as his sword. He has counseled sultans of different lands and guided us through challenges that I know I could have never imagined."

Zakee went back to his vizier and placed his hands on his shoulders. "This is a challenge beyond your knowledge, my friends. Changa is best equipped to handle it. I shall seek his counsel on this until we have vanquished the sheikh."

Changa nodded in time with Asif. Zakee had been more observant than he realized. He was handling Asif's concerns deftly.

The vizier tried to step away but Zakee held him firm. "You are a vital part of this plan. Mobilize our army and have them ready to march at first light. We must make good time. Who knows what awaits us in Sana'a."

Asif bowed deeply. "Yes, my sultan. I will do so immediately."

Asif hurried from the courtyard. Changa expected the cold glance he received but it was the second glance that raised his interest. The vizier's met those of Zakee's eldest sister, Khadeejah.

"Come, Changa," Zakee motioned. "I will show you where you will sleep."

Changa and the others followed Zakee across the courtyard and into the multi-leveled palace. The innards of the royal building were sparse when judged against comparable buildings in the Middle Kingdom and Vijyanagar but Zakee was not known to be a flamboyant person. The room he led them to was a large, spacious area filled with beds and weapon racks.

"It is the barracks for my personal guard," Zakee said. "I apologize for the inconvenience. It is all I could come up with in such a short time."

"Come now, Zakee," Changa said. "It's far more room than

below the Kazuri's deck. It'll do for one night."

The *Kazuri* baharia waded into the room, chiding each other as they chose their beds. Changa and the Tuareg were about to follow when Zakee raised his hand.

"My brothers, you will come with me."

Changa frowned. "It's not our way, Zakee. You know this."

"I understand, Changa, but it is the Yemeni way. If Asif and the others see you sleeping here they will continue to believe you are my servants."

"It doesn't matter to us what they think," Changa responded.

"It matters to me." Zakee looked worried. "I need them to respect your counsel."

Changa looked at the Tuareg and saw understanding in his gaze.

"Lead us," Changa conceded.

A wide spiral staircase took them to the highest level of the palace. Here the wealth of the Basheer clan was on display. Zakee led them down an ornate hallway to a pair of elaborately carved doors accented with gold and jewel inlays.

"This is my bedroom," Zakee said, an embarrassed tone heavy in his voice. "It was once the room of my mother and father, but now that I am sultan I am forced to occupy it. These are your rooms."

He pointed to the doors opposite each other.

"They would usually be occupied by my vizier and my treasurer, but Asif has chosen to stay on the second level with my mother and sisters."

Changa noted the implications in Zakee's statement. The Tuareg nodded to them both and entered his room. Changa hesitated, held in place by Zakee's morose face.

"I see you're disappointed."

"I am," Zakee admitted. "This should be a time of celebration. Instead I am mourning my father's death and preparing for war. At times I think we should have sailed on."

"Eventually you would come home," Changa said. "This is not the way you wanted it to be but life never is. At least you have the chance to make life better for your people."

Zakee's face brightened. "Yes I do and you will help me." Changa smiled. "Get some rest. We march tomorrow."

Changa patted Zakee's shoulder before entering his room. It was a lavish chamber, a marble floor covered by an enormous Persian rug sprawling before him. The centerpiece was a huge canopy bed, its posts draped with thin silk covers. Each corner held a column pedestal crown with a golden unlit lamp. Patterned Persian carpets draped the plaster walls. Whatever this room was it definitely was not for a vizier or a treasurer. Changa suspected that if he guessed Zakee's father had concubines he would be correct.

A huge yawn broke through Changa's focus. He trudged to the canopy bed, kicked off his shoes then fell asleep. It seemed only moments when a commotion outside his door roused him.

"Zakee, open the door. It is Asif and Khadeejah."

Changa was halfway to the door when he heard Zakee's portal open. The voices were not clear as the three exchanged pleasantries; by the time Changa reached his door the trio had retired into Zakee's room. Changa opened the door and met the curious stare of the Tuareg.

"It seems those two are not thoroughly convinced of our intentions," Changa commented.

The Tuareg nodded

"Tomorrow I want you to keep an eye on Khadeejah. There's more to her than she reveals."

Changa was tempted to enter the room and demand to know what was being said but thought better of it. Zakee was honest to a fault. He was sure he'd be told tomorrow.

He went back into his room and succumbed to the voluptuous comfort of the canopy bed.

2

A Bonding Moment

Changa awoke to an insistent rapping on his door.

"Alright!" he shouted. He threw on his pants and shirt and stomped to the door. When he snatched it open the startled servant almost fell into him.

"Your breakfast, sir," he stammered. Changa made way for a procession of servants carrying tables and trays. A similar spectacle took place across the hall in the Tuareg's room and to his right in Zakee's room. The last member of the processional surprised him; it was Khadeejah.

"Good morning, Changa," she said sweetly. "I hope you rested well."

Changa watched her as she walked past and sat before his breakfast table. He joined her, a suspicious look on his face.

"I decided to save you the trouble," she said. She removed her veil, startling him. It was Muslim custom that no one sees the face of a woman except the family or her husband and Changa was neither. Her face was a bit thin for Changa's likes but attractive nonetheless.

"My brother considers you family so I will respect his wishes," she continued.

"Please, eat. You must have your strength when you leave."

"So why are you here?" Changa asked.

Khadeejah's face became stern. "It was a happy day when Zakee returned, but it was a sad day as well. Zakee is my favorite brother. It angered me when he chose to marry that Zanj whore and leave our land. I will also admit I was not happy when he returned in the company of people who resemble those who stole him from us. But it seems your intentions are good and he cares for you greatly. My worry is if those feelings are reciprocated."

Changa swallowed a mouthful of food before answering. "A dhow is a small craft, even when it is large. Men spend months together in close quarters. There is no room for secrets. Your crew is your survival for the sea is dangerous, especially to those who love her. Even if serving on a dhow doesn't make you love your fellow crewman it forges a bond that goes beyond emotions. Zakee served on my smallest dhow, the Kazuri. The men who serve with him think of him as a brother and that's why they are here. They protect their own and I protect them."

Khadeejah nodded but still didn't seem convinced. Changa didn't care.

"Zakee has no need to fear us. He knows this. But where he sees family I see vipers waiting to strike."

"You insult us!" Khadeejah shrieked.

Changa continued to eat. "Do I? Zakee has been warned of his brothers, but no one has warned him about Asif…and you."

"Asif is a loyal servant as he has always been," Khadeejah spat.

"How much of his loyalty is due to your favors?" Changa asked.

Khadeejah's hand flashed at Changa's face and he caught her wrist and squeezed. Khadeejah grimaced and she fell back into her seat.

"I don't know what your intentions are and I don't care," Changa explained. "I only know that when I leave Aden…if I leave Aden…Zakee will be in control and he will be surrounded by those are truly loyal to him. If I were you I would make sure I was among the loyal."

Changa let her wrist go and she jerked her hand back. She rubbed her wrist before replacing her veil.

"My loyalty to Zakee is beyond reproach, as is Asif's. I hope your journey is safe, at least for my brother. Goodbye, bwana Diop."

Khadeejah hurried from his room and almost crashed into Zakee and the Tuareg.

"Khadeejah!" Zakee exclaimed. "What are you doing here?"

Khadeejah didn't answer. She cut a final glance at Changa

and stormed away.

Zakee came to Changa with a worried look. The Tuareg's eyes were just as concerned.

"Changa, what was my sister doing in your room?"

Changa smiled at Zakee's implications.

"Don't worry, your sister's virtue is in no harm from me. She joined me for breakfast. She is concerned about you."

"You would think I am a child!" Zakee pouted. "I have seen more of the world than any of them."

"Don't be harsh. They see you as you were when they last saw you. They don't know you as we do."

"Still, I am sultan now. They should respect my word."

Changa stared at Zakee, disappointed by his statement. He stood and donned his weapons with a frown.

"Receiving a gaudy knife from your mother may have given you a title but it doesn't give you respect. You were chosen to be sultan. Now you must prove you deserve it."

Changa brushed by Zakee roughly as he exited his room and marched down the hall, the Tuareg by his side.

"I am sorry," Zakee said. "It's just frustrating that everyone thinks of me as some ignorant child…even you."

Changa slowed and Zakee came to his side. "I know what you're capable of. You will make a great sultan. But now you must be vigilant. Your sultanate is at war and your people are waiting to see who will emerge the victor. Not just between you and the Red Sheikh but you and your brothers. You'll have to keep those around you close but distant until you know their motives."

Zakee nodded. "I understand, Changa. I will try."

They entered the courtyard, the shadow of the nearby mountains delaying the morning light. The chill of the desert night still clung to the air as the clamor of the market drifted over the palace walls. Asif's rescue force assembled before them in ragged lines and with groggy faces. It was a sorry sight. The garrison was the most promising, standing in perfect rank, shining conical helmets on their heads, scimitars at their sides and lances gripped in their hands. They were flanked by the militia, a rough looking group whose garments and weapons were as varied as their dispositions. Changa couldn't be too judgmental when it came to appearances; his *Kazuri* baharia were just as varied. The difference was he knew exactly what they were capable of.

The nobles formed their horsemen, flanking both sides of the foot soldiers. They were resplendent in their flowing robes and headscarves, their armed servants decked in shining armor and new blades. If he was a farmer's daughter he'd be impressed.

Lastly there was the Turkomen, Asif's homeland mercenaries. They sat upon tall, upright *Akhalteke* horses, elegant beasts bred to look long across the deserts and grasslands from where they came. Their riders wore white round hats of fur that matched their pants; they wore red long sleeved shirts that covered their knees. They reminded Changa of the Mongols. If they were anything like his old allies they were a formidable force.

"I hope the Red Sheikh is on his heels," he commented. "My confidence is not lifted by this group."

"They are good fighters," Zakee defended. "Many of the nobles marched with my father into the north to quell the desert tribes. The garrison may not be war tested but they are brave and loyal men. As for the mercenaries, their reputation is strong. Asif assures me they will do their duty to the upmost."

Asif arrived immediately after Zakee mentioned his name. He bowed his head to Zakee then glanced at Changa.

"Sultan, we are ready to depart."

Zakee mounted his horse. "Changa, Panya, and Asif, you will ride with me. The Kazuri baharia will ride as my personal guard. Asif, your Turkomen will take their place behind them. The rest of the army will follow with the exception of the scouts. I want them at least a mile ahead of us."

Asif seemed stunned by Zakee's firm orders. A smile came to him soon afterward.

"As you command, Sultan!" He spurred his horse and galloped away, shouting orders as he went. Changa and the Tuareg pulled alongside him.

"How did I do?" Zakee asked.

"Excellent," Changa replied. "I don't agree with you riding in the lead, however. You'll be too much of a target."

"I must take the risk," Zakee replied. "The Yemeni expect me to lead them."

"It will also make it harder to keep you alive, which will be no different than when you're on the Kazuri," Changa chided.

They were laughing when Panya rode up. Their humor made her smile, which in turn brought a wider smile to Changa's face.

She guided her horse alongside Zakee then extended a small leather pouch to him. The young sultan pulled away.

"What is this?"

"You know what it is. It will protect you."

Zakee looked at the bag as if it was a foreign object. Changa took the bag from Panya.

"Now is not the time," he said to Panya. "Zakee's people would look down on him if they see him accepting it. He will take it later."

"Changa, you know how I feel about such things," Zakee said.

Changa frowned. "These 'things' have saved you and me more than once. Keep your beliefs but take this bag when it is more convenient."

Zakee nodded but Changa guessed the discussion was not over. He hid the bag in his shirt as Asif returned.

"We are ready, Sultan."

"Then let us be off," Zakee announced. "My brothers await our relief."

The commotion on the merchant city was usurped by blaring trumpets stationed along the ramparts. Melodic voices emanated from the city's minarets, joining the martial call. Zakee lifted his head and spurred his horse to the gates. The procession began slowly as the warriors took their place and followed the royal entourage through the streets. Merchants, pedestrians, workers, and idlers turned their attention to the army. Curious mumbling evolved into raucous cheers as the marchers' intent became obvious to the onlookers.

"Break the siege at Sana'a!"

"Free our brothers!"

"Defeat the infidel Red Sheikh!"

"Allah praise Sultan Zakee!"

Zakee raised his hand and waved at the crowd. Changa rode stoically, his face an emotionless mask. It was easy to be taken in by the enthusiasm of an adoring crowd. But soon the crowd would fail and the road would remain. What waited at the end of that road was what kept him sober.

The crowd could still be heard in the distance as Zakee's relief force reached the base of the mountains. A steep road snaked into the barren rocks, a dismal sight for men so long at sea. The army marched briskly into the dingy peaks but soon found their energy spent. The city garrison were neophytes to long marches and tired quickly. Only the Turkomen seemed unfazed, but they were nomads and they were used to the rigors of the road. They made camp at the first site large enough to hold their numbers.

"Send out scouts to assess the road ahead," Changa advised. "Give the men a few minutes to rest their legs then get them going again. The longer we linger the more the situation changes in Sana'a."

Asif's face turned red. "It is the sultan who gives the orders here!"

Zakee smiled. "Changa is doing what he is here for. You are a great administrator but Changa has knowledge in these matters."

"He is a merchant!" Asif exclaimed. "What does he know of war?"

"Far more than I'd like," Changa replied. "I would gladly turn this responsibility over to you, Asif, if I thought you were capable of handling it. You are an intelligent man and I'm sure in time you would make a great strategist. But we don't have time. You tend to your mercenaries and I'll get us to Sana'a."

"And how will you do that, general?" Asif's expression became smug. "You know nothing of Yemen."

"That's true," Changa admitted. "That's why you'll pick your most knowledgeable men and send them out to scout."

Asif snarled then stormed off.

"Must you aggravate him so?" Zakee asked.

"He causes his own aggravation," Changa said with a shrug. He looked about the camp and saw Panya wandering into the hills, the Tuareg close behind. At least one person didn't have to be told their duties. Their eyes met and she smiled.

"Get comfortable and enjoy the moment, Zakee. You'll never get this much attention from me again."

Zakee laughed. "I must say I'm actually enjoying ordering you about."

"Don't make me hit you."

Changa met Panya and the Tuareg at the base of the slopes.

"What do you see?" he asked the priestess.

"The sheikh's presence is not strong here," she replied. "He has spies in Aden and he surely knows we've departed for Sana'a."

"He may try to take the city before we arrive, not that we're much of a relief force," Changa mused.

"Or he may wait until all the brothers are present before attacking," Panya added. "If he can kill all three he will eliminate the succession and throw the sultanate into turmoil."

"Maybe we should have remained in Aden and forced him to come to us," Changa wondered aloud.

"Zakee wouldn't have agreed," Panya said. "I think he feels there is some chance of reconciliation with his brothers."

"I wish he was right but I know he's wrong." Changa looked at his friends with concern. "We'll have to stay close to him. He's going to have to do some things that will upset him greatly."

Panya and the Tuareg nodded in agreement.

"We'll give everyone a little while longer then we'll set out again as soon as Asif's scouts return."

Half the day passed before Changa realized the scouts were not returning. He went immediately to Zakee, Asif close behind.

"We're in danger," Changa said. "Someone is waiting for us ahead."

"How do you know?" Asif asked. "My scouts haven't returned."

"Exactly." Changa began pacing. "If they were smart they would have let the scouts return and ambushed us later. The fact that they killed the scouts proves that they're probably bandits who got anxious. Still it's an obstacle we can't afford."

He turned to Asif. "Are bandits common in these hills?"

"Somewhat, but they would save their blades for easier prey. They would be foolish to harass an army."

"Foolish or confident." Changa nodded at Zakee. "I insist that you ride in the center for the remainder of this journey. If anyone needs to reach Sana'a alive it's you. Asif, I want half of your mercenaries to the front and the remainder in the rear. There will be no more scouts; we can't afford to lose any more men. We move slowly and we stay diligent."

Asif did not protest Changa's orders. The death of the scouts seemed to rattle him for he almost stumbled when he rushed from Zakee's presence. Changa looked at Zakee, a grim smile on his face.

"It seems our part in this war has begun."

The rescue army broke camp and proceeded cautiously. Changa's orders were followed; the mercenaries led them through the winding paths, their sharp eyes scanning broken rocks and shrub stands. The garrison troops studied the landscape as well but their untrained eyes were useless. Changa and the baharia formed a tight circle around Zakee, their crossbows strapped to their backs, their bolt sacks on their hips. Changa rode ahead of the sultan for a moment then slowed his mount to come beside him. He slipped Panya's pouch into his robe. Zakee opened his mouth to protest but Changa cut him off with a wave.

"Anyone or anything brave enough to attack an army is not ordinary," Changa said. "Don't take any chances."

The sun skimmed the crests of the peaks when the Turkomen leader suddenly raised his hand high. They were in a wide section of the road bordered by a grassy field, the wooded peaks a fair distance away. The baharia took the crossbows from their backs; Changa moved his horse close to Zakee as Panya and the Tuareg approached. The look on Panya's face told him what he needed to know.

"This is no ordinary attack," Changa shouted. "Be…"

A high pitch scream drowned his words. A group of garrison troops a few feet away tumbled into a pile as something heavy landed among them. The men screamed as they scrambled away, trying to escape instead of fighting for their lives. Something chased after them, a pale misshapen thing resembling a man in the vaguest way. Its face was faint as if it was burned away, leaving nose slits and a lipless maw. Its thin body possessed strength far beyond its physical appearance, which it demonstrated by lifting one of the soldiers by the arm and flinging it into the others like a small rock. The entire army was set to flee in chaos until a Turkomen rode before the beast and drove his lance into its gut, pinning the beast to the ground. He jumped from his horse, snatched out his sword then hacked its neck. His second strike cut the man-beast's head free from its deformed body.

The mercenary glared at the others before climbing back onto his mount and returning to the ranks of his comrades just as a chorus of shrieks swarmed from the grass. Changa leaped off his horse and waded through the garrison troops.

"Raise your lances!" he shouted. "Archers behind the lancers!"

The garrison troops scrambled to get in position as the source of the shrieks burst from the grass. A hideous mass of deformed humanity charged them, the obvious fruit of demented magic. Scores of man-beasts hopped, ran and stumbled at them, shrieking and bellowing as they approached. Soldiers and nobles turned their terrified faces at the one man among them who seemed unaffected by the horrific onslaught. Changa held his Damascus in his right hand and a throwing knife in his left, his stoic face masking the nervousness inside. Could there be a tebo among the creatures? He'd thought he escaped Usenge's underlings when he sailed to the Middle Kingdom but they had found him in the wastelands of Mongolia. He had no encounters in Vijyanagar but he was closer to his homeland and the sorcerer had proven that his reach was great, no matter how sporadic. He gripped his knife tightly, the only weapon that seemed to be able to stop the beasts marked for him, and he waited.

Screams of men and beasts mingled as the monsters attacked the line. A score of beasts rose over the front ranks and the archers fired, riddling the creatures in mid-flight. Changa threw his knife at a beast that avoided the fusillade, striking it in the head. The troops scattered to let the bodies hit the ground then impaled them with angry spear thrusts. While the left flank held its own, the right flank crumbled. Soldiers fled, dropping their weapons so they could run faster. The reason for their headlong flight appeared through the dust like a familiar nightmare. Changa cursed as he jerked his throwing knife from the dead beast's head and confronted the massive creature meant only for him.

The tebo had no need to hide its true form among its deformed companions. It ran gorilla-like at Changa, its thick hands striking the ground while its short legs pounded beneath it. There its resemblance to the noble forest beast ended. Its bare skin writhed over misshapen muscles as it opened its mouth, exposing sharp, jagged teeth. Instead of two arms the beast flailed four appendages, the third protruding from the middle of its chest, the fourth reaching over its shoulder from its back. Changa sheathed his sword and took another knife from his waist belt. The finely crafted blade was no use against a tebo; only the mystic iron in the shape of his throwing blades could kill the beast, and even then those blades had to be in the hands of one who possessed the royal blood of Kongo.

"Everyone get away!" Changa shouted. "This one has come for me."

The soldiers gladly obeyed Changa's command. The relief from confronting the massive beast spurred their efforts against the other creatures. They attacked them fearlessly, driving them back into the grasslands. Changa and the tebo circled each other, their eyes locked. This one seemed more intelligent than the others he'd confronted earlier. It was cautious where its slain cohorts were more aggressive.

"Why must you fight, son of Mfumu?" Its voice attacked him, weaving a feeling of despair within his head. "Your father awaits you among the ancestors. Give yourself to me and your suffering will cease."

Changa answered by throwing his knife. The tebo moved, but not fast enough. The blade bit into its shoulder and the tebo moaned. Changa tried to move in with his second knife poised to strike but the tebo lashed out with its right arm, knocking Changa into a spin. His knife flew from his hand; before he could scramble to it the tebo grabbed his ankle with its chest hand and dragged him away. The knife was out of reach. His only other knife rested in the tebo's bleeding shoulder. Changa stopped struggling and let the tebo drag him close. It grabbed him with its other hand, bring him face to face. Changa winced in its tight grip, its hot, putrid breath seeping through its fangs. The tebo opened its maw as it reached for Changa with its other hands. Changa kicked with his free leg, striking the beast's chin. Its mouth slammed shut, the force cracking a few teeth. The tebo's grip loosened on Changa's other leg and he pulled it free. Bringing both legs together he kicked the tebo's face repeatedly. The creature stumbled backwards with each blow until it lost its balance and fell, crushing some of its distorted comrades beneath it. It lost its grip on the Bakonga; Changa landed atop of it just above its breast arm. He crawled frantically to his knife then yanked the blade free from the tebo's shoulder. Then he pounced, landing on the tebo's chest as he drove the knife into its throat. Cold black blood spurted into his face as he pushed the blade deeper until the tebo shuddered and fell still. Changa pulled the knife free and slid off the beast's body to the grass

The Tuareg appeared before him, the bottom of his dingy blue pants coming into Changa's view. Changa looked up into his friend's masked face and took his extended hand. As he stood a cheer erupted among the men, each one waving his weapon over his head and shouting. Zakee ran to him and Asif followed.

"We have our first victory!" Zakee exclaimed. "Allah be praised!"

Asif approached him with wide eyes and mouth agape.

"See to your mercenaries," Changa said. "We'll bury the dead and move on. This thing gives off a terrible stink."

"Yes, Changa," Asif said.

Changa placed a stern eye on Zakee. "What are you doing here without the baharia?"

Zakee grinned and Changa grinned back. The young sultan struck a regal pose and his Swahili brothers surrounded him. They made no commotion about Changa's defeat of the tebo for they had witnessed him do much more. It would have surprised them if he failed.

While Asif called the mercenaries to order, the Tuareg silently reformed the garrison soldiers. Changa felt a light touch and looked to his left into Panya's worried stare.

"Let me look at you," she said.

"I'm fine," he replied.

Panya grabbed his shoulders and turned him to face her. "No you're not. I know you, Changa Diop. That was a great show you put on but I know different. Sit down."

Changa obeyed. Panya took his face between her hands and stared into his eyes. A slight smile came to her face before her hands roamed his body. She frowned whenever he winced.

"Minor wounds," he commented.

"Nothing is minor from a spirit beast," she answered. She reached into her medicine pouch and took out a small gourd.

"Drink this."

Changa drank the bitter solution. While it burned its way to his gut Panya took out another gourd and spread ointment on his wounds.

"Will you tend to the others?"

"No," she replied. "We have healers enough for them. You are my concern. That's why you hired me, remember?"

She looked up for a moment and this time gave him a full smile.

Changa felt relief, but he wasn't sure if it was from the elixir or Panya's changing attitude.

The army moved away from the grim battleground, trudging another three miles before camping for the night. Tents littered the road and the bordering scrubland; soldiers, mercenaries and baharia gathered around numerous fires tending their wounds and discussing the weird battle. Zakee's tent was no different than the others, another insistence by Changa.

Changa, Panya, Zakee, the Tuareg, and Asif sat before their own fire, roasting a wild goat brought down by a lucky bahari. The mood among them ranged from stoic to exuberant, the latter emotion radiating from Zakee's bright face.

"The men fought well," he commented. "They were frightened at first but they found their strength in your example, Changa."

Changa shrugged as he sliced a piece of goat. "The Turkomen did better than I expected. Asif, I must apologize to you. Your brothers are formidable warriors."

"It is I that must apologize to you," Asif replied. "The baharia formed an impenetrable wall around the sultan, and your battle with the giant beast was unbelievable. Long ago I trusted Sultan Zakee's judgment. It seems I must learn to do so again."

"How far are we from Sana'a?" Panya asked.

"Three days at the most," Asif replied.

"We'll rest a day before continuing," Changa decided. "I hate losing the time but we need the rest. Sana'a must wait another day."

3

A Grim Reunion

The noon day sun hovered over the beleaguered city of Sana'a, its heat tempered by the cool altitude. The guards patrolling the southern walls ambled in a half trance across the pitted stone, barely paying attention to the wood slopes beyond them. It was the north from where the sheikh would come. Their duty was token at best, punishment at the worst. No threat would come from the direction of Aden.

Still, they were startled into fear when the sultan's vanguard appeared over the horizon. They ran about frantically, waving their weapons and yelling into the city. A din of drums and horns sounded moments later; the gate opened and a squad of armored horsemen with battered lances and ragged banners galloped to them.

Changa nodded to the Tuareg and Asif. They broke away from Zakee's ring and rode to the head of the relief force, meeting the city outriders a few yards ahead of the group. One of the outriders approached them, a stout man with a frowning face.

"What is this?" he demanded. "Sultan Wazeer did not request reinforcements!"

Asif's eyes narrowed. "Wazeer is no sultan. We have come to relieve Sana'a under the orders of the true sultan, Zakee ibn Basheer!"

Zakee rode forward, maneuvering his mount between Changa and Asif. The *Kazuri* baharia and Turkomen galloped forward as well, forming a semi-circle around the city guard.

Zakee raised his father's jambiya. "I am Zakee ibn Basheer, Son of Basheer and Sultan of Yemen."

The guardsman reluctantly bowed to Zakee. "I beg your pardon…sultan. My men and I will lead you to Sana'a."

The Aden relief force followed the Sana'a force into the city. The stench assailed Changa as soon as the gates swung wide. The city was filled with filth, the obvious sign of siege. Changa realized why they'd been allowed into the city and he cursed. He looked at the Tuareg and his suspicions were confirmed by his concerned gaze.

Two men in fine robes stormed toward them followed by two ranks of soldiers. One man stood a head taller than Changa and almost as wide. His thick beard almost covered his entire lower face, the rest shadowed by his thick brow. The other man ran to keep up, his robes hanging off his thin frame. His face was clean shaven except for a thin moustache crowning his equally thin lips.

"You're damn fools, all of you!" the larger man shouted. His eyes looked upon Zakee, Changa, and the others then focused on Asif.

"Who authorized this, Asif? My mother?"

"I did, Wazeer." Zakee rode forward and dismounted. Wazeer glared for a moment then his eyes widened. He jerked his head up to Zakee's face then down to the jeweled jambiya.

"Zakee?" It was the other man who spoke. He rushed Zakee, his arms outstretched. Changa intervened, placing his bulk between his friend and his brother.

"Call off your Zanj," Khalid snapped.

Changa bristled at the way Khalid spat the word, his hand seeking his throwing knife.

Wazeer came forward and was blocked by the Tuareg. He eyed the blue robed man then stepped away.

"So you are alive," Wazeer commented.

"Changa, Tuareg, please let my brothers through," Zakee asked.

Changa and the Tuareg stepped aside. Zakee held his arms opened then embraced Wazeer. Their hug was perfunctory, Wazeer looking over his long lost brother's shoulder at the army gathered behind him. His hug with Khalid seemed genuine. Khalid struck his back with brotherly affection then leaned back to look at Zakee's face.

"Allah has brought you back to us," he announced.

"He has," Zakee agreed. "I have come to help you."

"We did not need your help," Wazeer said. "All you have done is entered a trap. Now the sheikh has all of us. The fruit of Basheer will die together."

Zakee looked at Changa with questioning eyes.

"He may be right," Changa said. "This is a city under siege yet we encountered no opposition except the beasts in the mountains."

Wazeer and Khalid looked startled. "You defeated the beasts?"

Changa grinned. "Of course."

"Then the siege is broken!" Wazeer shouted. "We don't have much time. Khalid, tell our officers to spread the word. We will evacuate before sundown."

"We are not leaving," Zakee said.

Wazeer took a stance before Zakee. "You don't understand little brother. Your victory was temporary. Those same creatures you slew today will be back among the living in a short time. They will block the road again. We must hurry."

"No," Zakee said, this time with the force of authority in his voice. "If we give up Sana'a then the sheikh has a clear road to Aden."

"It seems we must decide who leads here," Wazeer said. He stepped back, his right hand grasping the hilt of his jambiya. Changa's hand found his Damascus.

"No, Changa," Asif warned. "Do not interfere. You know what must happen."

"I won't allow Zakee to be harmed."

Asif nodded. "I understand. But a people cannot serve two sultans."

Zakee reluctantly sought the hilt of his father's dagger. "I hold our father's jambiya in my hand. It is a symbol of my birthright and his power. It was given to me by our mother who followed our father's wishes."

"Neither you nor our mother was there when our father died," Wazeer retorted. "I held his head as he took his last breath. He gave me his blessing and his inheritance. When I came back from the battle I told mother this and she refused to believe me. She fled with our sisters and the jambiya."

Zakee turned to Khalid. "Is what he saying true, brother?"

Khalid looked at Zakee, then at Wazeer, then at Zakee again.

"I cannot say," he finally admitted. "It is true Wazeer was with father when he died. What was said between them I cannot confirm because I was too far away to hear. I only know what Wazeer told me."

Wazeer glared at Khalid. His expression did not change when his eyes came back to Zakee.

"It does not matter. The men in this city take orders from me. Here, I am sultan."

Changa frowned at Zakee's silence. This was a crucial moment for Zakee and the rest of them.

"I can't allow that," Zakee finally said. He unsheathed his jambiya.

Wazeer eyes narrowed. He pulled out his dagger as well. Khalid stared at both of them with wide eyes then stepped away as his brothers circled each other. There was a commotion behind Wazeer and Changa began to pull his Damascus free.

"No!" Asif barked. He gestured and Changa saw drummers emerge from the ranks. They formed a circle around the brothers and played a steady rhythm that complimented their hypnotic voices. Changa looked about the courtyard, assessing the situation. It was no doubt he could escape if things went wrong but he was unsure about the others. Panya moved close to him and his eyes met the Tuareg's. Their fate was in the hands of Zakee.

Wazeer launched a blistering attack at his young brother. His skills were amazing, the dagger flicking at Zakee like a serpent's strike. If his brother had been the same youth Changa stumbled upon in the forest he would be dead. But the man facing Wazeer had traveled to the limits of the Trade Lands, gaining a wealth of martial experience along the way. He parried and dodged his brother's lethal moves with equal alacrity. Sparks flew when their daggers clashed. Changa watched Zakee, a grim smile on his face. The Tuareg had taught him well. He was conserving his energy, letting his brother waste his anger and his strength with his increasingly wild attacks. It was a strategy used when you only want to disarm or defeat an opponent, not kill him.

Wazeer hesitated, his skills spent. Zakee pounced, pressing his tired brother with a combination of blade, fists, and feet. Bruised and bleeding, Wazeer launched one last desperate attack. His sudden lunge almost caught Zakee off guard. His initial stumble backwards was genuine; his extra steps were planned. When Wazeer was fully committed Zakee sidestepped and swept his brother's feet. Wazeer face smacked the ground; Zakee sat on his brother's back then grabbed a handful of his hair. He jerked Wazeer's head back and put his blade on his throat.

"I will not kill you if you concede," Zakee said. "We must join together to defeat the sheikh. Will you concede?"

Wazeer closed his eyes. "Yes."

Changa shook his head as did the Tuareg. This was not over. Best deal with him at that moment than later, Changa thought.

Zakee let his brother go and dismounted him. As he walked back to his entourage Wazeer jumped to his feet and rushed toward Zakee's back. He was quick, but Changa was quicker.

"Zakee!" he shouted.

Zakee dropped instinctively and the throwing knife whizzed over his head then plunged into Wazeer's forehead. Wazeer stood for a moment then collapsed.

Wazeer's men surged toward Zakee and his army. Khalid placed himself between them.

"No!" he shouted. "Wazeer violated his oath! You heard him concede. What use is it to serve a dead man? Zakee is our sultan. We obey him now!"

Wazeer's followers shuffled about passing unsure glances back and forth. Khalid turned to Zakee. He glanced at Changa then to his younger brother. He dropped to one knee, pulled out this jambiya and offered it over his head.

"I am your servant, brother." A small contingent of men, Khalid's men, immediately repeated his gesture. Wazeer's men did so slowly, many of them cutting mean glances at Changa. He was unmoved. It wasn't the first time a large group of men wanted him dead and it certainly wouldn't be the last. He would have to watch himself.

"Sheath your dagger, brother," Zakee said softly. "We must bury our brother."

"No!" Khalid blurted. "His body must be burned immediately."

Zakee frowned. "You know we don't burn our dead."

Khalid stood, his face resolved. "We do now, at least in Sana'a. The dead belong to the Red Sheikh."

"What are you talking about?"

Khalid signaled Wazeer's men and they gathered his body. "It is the reason we have not been able to defeat him. The Red Sheikh has the power to bring his slain warriors back from the dead. We kill them one day and the next day they stand before us again. Even our own dead stand among them, their minds empty, their bodies manipulated by his evil. The desert folk flock to him with his promises of immortality, but they do not realize the truth of his promise."

Zakee eyes were wide with shock. "What of our father?"

Khalid looked away. "By the time he was slain we knew what the sheikh could do. We brought him into the citadel to burn him but our mother refused. He was given a traditional burial. The next day a terrible sound came from his grave. We watched as he dug himself out and stumbled toward the gate. We could not let the sheikh claim him so we doused him with oil and set him afire. Mother left that same day, cursing us both and vowing never to return."

Panya stood by Changa's side, taking in Khalid's morbid tale.

"He is either a powerful sorcerer or has one serving him," she said.

"Can you kill him?" Zakee asked.

"No," Panya conceded. "I am too far from Oya to summon the power needed. I could weaken him, but I would have to be close to him. It would take someone with a special strength to finish the deed."

She ended her words looking at Changa. He looked away to hide the uneasiness in his chest. Panya referred to Kintu's Gift, the essence of the demi-god shared with Changa and the others in their battle against Bahati. Though its effect quickly dissipated among the others it lingered in Changa, appearing when he needed it most. Changa's life and the lives of the others benefitted from the mysterious force but Changa did not trust it. He had no idea how long the Gift would stay with him or when it would fail.

"So we must go to this sheikh and kill him?" Changa asked.

"Yes," Panya answered. "It is the only way."

"Our army must rest," Zakee decided. "The Red Sheikh's stronghold is probably a long journey and we must be at our best strength."

"No, brother," Khalid replied. "You cannot reach the sheikh's lair. You will have to break the siege to do so and even with your reinforcements we don't have the manpower to do it. The only reason the sheikh has not overrun Yemen is because we hold him here waiting on Allah's intervention."

Changa looked at the men of the city, paying close attention to Khalid's men.

"For the son of a sultan you have a small army," he concluded.

"My warriors are still at my compound," Khalid said. "Wazeer thought it prudent to keep them in reserve. When we finally needed them we couldn't get word to them."

Changa folded his arms across his chest. "Panya and I will deal with this sheikh. We'll need a guide."

Khalid laughed. "You say this as if it is an easy task. Haven't you listened to anything I said?"

"Yes I have and I've heard enough. Zakee, we'll launch a diversionary attack on the sheikh's army. Panya and I will slip through the lines and go after the sheikh. Send another contingent to Khalid's citadel and summon his troops. Have them march to

Sana'a but to stay out of distance until the time is right."

"And when will I know when the time is right?" Zakee asked.

Changa grinned. "I have no idea."

Sana'a reeled with the sudden change in events. Wazeer's men took his body to a corner section of the courtyard reserved for cremations. Zakee and Khalid followed; both brothers' faces reflections of despondence. Panya, the Tuareg, and Changa walked close together.

"Tuareg, stay close to Zakee. He is not safe. Wazeer's men cannot be trusted until this sheikh thing is done."

"What about Khalid?" Panya asked.

"He seems to want nothing of the sultanate," Changa replied. "His loyalty goes to the strongest and there's no one left but Zakee."

"There is Asif," she commented.

Changa shrugged. "He's loyal to Zakee and his sister. We need not worry about him. Our biggest challenge will be the sheikh. What will you need?"

"I have what I need," Panya replied.

Changa nodded. "Then all we need is a guide."

Wazeer's remains were taken to a charred pit near the citadel cemetery. As the bearers lowered the body into the pit a breeze stirred the dust and the warriors looked about nervously. Panya gripped Changa's arm.

"The sheikh comes to claim his prize!"

Khalid ran to the pit's edge. "Hurry, bring the wood!"

The men scrambled to the woodpile as the wind rapidly increased, swirling the dirt and dust about them. Changa squinted as he and Panya joined Khalid. Zakee stood with them as well, his face horrified.

"This is the Red Sheikh's doing?" he yelled over the wind.

"This is how he comes," Khalid shouted back. "But never has he come this strong!"

A sound came from within the pit, a mournful cry that shook Changa's bones. He looked into the hole and to his disgust saw Wazeer's body stir. Zakee stumbled away; Khalid cupped his hands over his mouth.

"Hurry!" he shouted.

The wood bearers were running for the pit as Wazeer attempted to stand. Panya pushed everyone aside as she yanked a pouch from her waist belt.

"No!" Khalid shouted. "Do not foul my brother's body with your blasphemy!"

The wind twisted tighter around the pit. Wazeer's corpse became more animated, stiff hands pushing at the tight wrapping from within. Streams of dust attacked the wood bearers, stinging their eyes and hands, forcing them to drop their wood and cover their faces.

Panya tried to approach the pit's edge but Khalid obstructed her.

"I said..."

Changa rushed Khalid, punching the man across the jaw then catching his unconscious body before he hit the ground. He lifted Khalid onto his shoulder.

"Do it," he said.

Panya took out the leather bag and grabbed a handle of the concoction.

"Oya help me," she whispered.

She flung the powder which fell onto Wazeer despite the whirlwind. The body stiffened the collapsed, shaking weakly at the pit bottom.

Changa turned to the baharia. "Bring the wood now!"

The baharia broke ranks and picked up the wood. They rushed to the pit and piled it on Wazeer's writhing body. The Tuareg appeared with a flaming torch and nonchalantly tossed it into the pit. Changa imagined that if the Tuareg did not wear his face veil he would have spat into the pit as well.

The fire spread quickly, enhanced by Panya's powder. The heat from the intense blaze pushed them back from the pit's edge.

Changa was walking to Panya with Khalid still on his shoulder when a gust of wind shoved him aside. He fell, Khalid tumbling from his shoulder. Panya's face grew fearful for a moment then she closed her eyes just before a violent tempest of wind and sand engulfed her. Changa scrambled from the ground then ran to her.

"Panya!"

Changa lunged at the swirling mass and was stung by the angry debris. Panya shouted over the roar and he was suddenly engulfed a burst of sand that flattened him on his back. The wind dispersed as quickly as it had come; Changa climbed to his feet. Panya stood before him, her arms spread and her eyes closed. She raised her head slowly and looked into Changa's eyes, a smirk forming on her face.

She sauntered to him and began knocking sand from his clothes.

"Are you okay?" Changa asked.

"I am Oya's daughter," she answered. "Wind cannot be used against me. The Red Sheikh knows that now."

The others gathered around Changa and Panya and the burning pit. Zakee looked at the fire consuming his brother's body in anger. He strode to the others.

"When will you be ready to depart?"

"We need at least a night's rest," Changa answered. "And we still haven't found a guide."

"One night's rest," he said. "You will have your guide in the morning."

He began to leave then turned back. Gone was the strain in his face; the old Zakee seemed to have returned.

"Thank you both." He extended his arms and they fell into his hug.

They watched him walk away before speaking.

"What did you learn?" Changa asked Panya.

"He is powerful," she answered. "I'm lucky that I am close to Oya. In the Middle Kingdom I would have been consumed. We will have to be very careful, Changa. If Kintu's gift does not manifest in you we cannot defeat him."

"Our chances are not good then," he said.

"It is our only option," she answered.

Changa stood silent for a moment. He was not a man to go on a fool's errand. If the chance of them defeating the sheikh was slim he was not about to sacrifice himself. He would rather take Zakee and sail away. On the other hand he knew Zakee would not leave. He would not desert his homeland or his family. Neither would Changa.

"It seems we have until tomorrow to find a way to improve our odds."

"We won't find a solution here," Panya warned. "If there was something or someone of power in Sana'a I would have sensed it by now."

"Maybe it is not magic we seek," Changa mused. "The Red Sheikh is human, is he not?"

"Yes."

"Then he will have more than one weakness. We'll have to find out what they are before we reach him."

Changa rested as much as he could through the night, which was not much. He feared no attack from the tebos; never had he been attacked twice by the creatures. But the happenings in Yemen unsettled him greatly. There were too many things going on, too many conspiracies swirling in addition to the looming threat of the Red Sheikh. Wazeer's death simplified matters but did not clear the threat to Zakee. He might not be able to clear all the conspiracies but he was determined not to leave until Zakee was safe.

4

THE SHEIKH'S SECRET

An uneasy night settled on Sana'a. In a matter of hours the city's command had turned over to a new sultan and a confrontation between two mysterious powers shook the nerves of the already desperate residents. So it was no surprise that Changa and Panya's efforts to question the fearful common folk resulted in nothing but blank stares or hostile words. They continued throughout the night with no success.

There was one bright spot, however. A guide was found, a person willing to lead them to the suspected lair of the sheikh. Changa sat in the guest chamber of the sultan's palace barely able to keep his eyes open. Panya paced beside him, her energy supplied by one of the many herbs she kept for such occasions. Changa had shared it as well but it was proving much less effective on him.

The chamber door creaked open and the Tuareg entered accompanied by a much smaller person covered in drab robes. Changa tried to make out his companion with his tired eyes but it was only when they drew near that he was able to discern at least the gender. It was a girl, her face covered by her dingy burka, her eyes darting back and forth between him and Panya. The Tuareg stopped as he neared and the girl walked forward and knelt before them.

"No need for that," Changa said in Arabic. "Who are you?"

"I am Ra'naa," she said. Her voice was thin and delicate.

"Why are you here?" Panya asked.

"Sultan Zakee said you were looking for a guide. I can take you to the Red Sheikh."

"You know these mountains well?" Changa asked.

"Very well. I grew up in them. I came to the city with the others as the sheikh began his war."

Panya suddenly stopped pacing. She knelt before the girl

and smiled.

"Give me your hand," she asked.

Changa watched intensely as the girl slowly extended her hand. Panya took it and closed her eyes.

"There is truth in her. But there is something else, too."

The girl jerked and tried to take her hand back. Panya held it firm.

"What else do you need to tell us?" Panya asked.

"Please, let go of my hand," she pleaded. "I will not run away."

Panya released her hand. Ra'naa stepped back and the Tuareg edged closer to her. She looked at him and stopped.

"I gave you my promise," she assured them. "I will take you directly to the Red Sheikh, but I ask a promise in return. I know you are a powerful sorceress, so I know my request is just a wish, but I will ask it anyway. When we find the Red Sheikh, I ask that you spare his life."

"That's impossible," Changa snapped.

Panya glared at Changa. "Why do you ask this, Ra'naa?"

"I know the Red Sheikh," the girl replied. "He is my father."

Ra'naa's words slapped Changa to full attention. Panya leaned back and gasped.

"He is not who you seek," the girl continued. "It is something inside him that controls him. He does not wish to do what he does. He has no choice."

Tears seeped from Ra'naa's eyes and Panya took her hand again.

"Tell us what happened," Panya whispered.

"My father was the headman of our village. He was a man of great faith and was well respected, even by those whose age demanded his respect. Two years ago the rains were scarce and our crops withered. For a time we did not suffer for my father had always urged us to keep the granaries full for times such as these. But as the months passed and the grain dwindled he became anxious and angry. At first he prayed, and then he accused other for not praying properly. He ordered us to pray together so he was sure that no one failed to meet their obligation. Still the grain diminished and the rains did not come. My father changed; he became desperate. One day he told my mother he was leaving to contemplate our situation alone. He was gone for a week. The first day my mother did not worry, but after a time her concern overcame her trust. She sent my older brothers out to find father but they returned alone. Just as the elders were organizing a search for him my father returned. He strode into our village with a confidence that seemed strange despite our predicament. There was something else different about him as well. He wore a red robe of the likes no one in our village had ever seen. It shimmered like clear water and felt smooth like a baby's skin."

"Silk," Changa said.

Ra'naa nodded. "That is what he called it. He gathered everyone and told us not to worry any longer. The rains would come soon and the granaries would be full again. He led us to a field of wild oats which we harvested in joy. Some of the villagers dropped to their knees to pray but my father stopped them.

"'You do not need to pray anymore,' he said.

"These were strange words coming from my father. Later that day my mother asked him what he meant and he would not answer her. He just smiled and stroked his robe.

"The rains came. We celebrated, certain my father was truly blessed. We attempted to pray and again he stopped us. There would be no more prayer, he said. We would bless ourselves with our own hands and our own actions. Many felt uncomfortable with his words but they obeyed. He had brought us food and rain. Who were we to question him?"

Ra'naa fell silent for a time. Changa became agitated waiting for her to continue, but Panya said nothing. After a time she embraced Ra'naa, cradling her head against her bosom.

"It is hard for a child to see a parent go wrong," Panya said. "It is even harder to accept it."

"I never would have if it hadn't been the way he began to treat mamma and the rest of us," Ra'naa answered. "Still, I think we all would have ignored his ways if it hadn't been for the sacrifice."

Changa's mood soured. A grim image from the past surfaced; the masked visage of Usenge. Panya seemed to sense his uneasiness for she looked toward him with a soft gaze.

"A year had passed and our village's vitality was restored. On the week of harvest my father announced we should celebrate our good fortune with a feast in his honor, for it was his wisdom and power that had brought us through such a hard time. In return for his help he asked that a sacrifice be made. He ordered the men of the village to go to the village nearest to us and capture their strongest man. That man would be killed in my father's honor. His strength would add to my father's so that he would be able to continue to nurture our prosperity.

"The elders protested vehemently but others complied. A man from a village nearby was captured then killed in my father's name. It was then my mother gathered us and left the village. We came to Sana'a."

"So how do you know this Red Sheikh is your father?" Changa asked.

Ra'naa looked at him. "I know."

"I must be truthful to you," Panya said. "I am not sure we can defeat the sheikh. The actions you describe suggest that something evil sits on your fathers head. We must drive it out to defeat it, but driving it out may mean hurting your father."

"Killing him, you mean," Ra'naa said.

Panya and Changa nodded their heads.

"If this thing has taken such a great hold on him then he is no longer my father and you will do what you must. But if there is a chance that his soul is still present..."

"We will do what we can," Changa said.

Ra'naa looked at them all with a hopeful smile. "Then I will take you to the Red Sheikh."

"Take her back home," Changa told the Tuareg. He knelt beside Ra'naa and Panya.

"We will come for you in the morning, little one. You will

have to be brave; this will not be an easy journey even if you do know the way. No one tried to stop you from leaving but they may try to stop you from returning."

"I will be ready," Ra'naa said.

Panya kissed her forehead before releasing her to the Tuareg. The two of them watched as Ra'naa and the Tuareg left the room.

"What do you think?" Changa asked.

"It sounds like a jinni," Panya replied. "Her father may have drawn its attention on his sojourn. A desperate man will answer to a jinni's plea even though he knows there is a price to pay."

Changa rubbed his chin. Djinns were powerful spirits.

"Can we defeat this jinni?"

"It depends. If Ra'naa's father's spirit remains we may have a chance. If not we can only trust in the ancestors."

Changa's interest could not hold back his fatigue. He yawned loudly, stretching his arms and flexing his fingers.

"This is all we can do for now. I must rest. We'll take this up in the morning."

Panya hesitated for a moment, then walked away to her room. Changa watched her, and then went inside.

5

AMONG THE DEAD

Changa's rest was short lived; he woke to the gentle shaking of the Tuareg's hand. Night caressed Sana'a with a temperate hand, brushing away the day's humid heat then laying a blanket of cool winds upon the nervous city. Changa accepted the woolen blanket offered to him by his friend, draping it over his broad shoulders and he left his room and entered the courtyard. The two of them climbed the closest rampart stairs and joined the chain of archers standing attentive, each training a keen eye on the wooded horizon. They continued around the ramparts until they met Zakee, Khalid, and Asif. All three men were grim faced; Khalid's expression seemed sharpened with a sense of worry.

"They should have come by now," he said.

"The night is early," Changa replied. "There's still time."

"No, Changa. The attack usually starts at dusk and continues until dawn. We sleep during the day and fight at night."

"How long has this gone on?" Zakee inquired.

"Two weeks," Khalid answered.

"Maybe they are resting," Asif surmised.

Khalid stared at Asif, his eyes narrow. "The dead need no rest. Something is wrong."

"Or something is right," Changa said. "We are here now. The garrison is reinforced and the sheikh must revise his strategy. He may be doing so this night which means we have a respite. I suggest we let these men rest and leave a few to stand guard. If he hasn't attacked by now he probably won't."

Khalid nodded. "You may be right. I will do as you ask."

He marched away, shouting orders in Arabic and Yemeni. The archers seemed reluctant to leave but eventually trailed away leaving only a few of their brethren on watch.

Zakee approached him. It was odd to see him in a sober mood, but the expression was becoming more common for him.

Changa smiled but Zakee's expression did not change.

"Did you speak with the girl?" he asked.

"Yes," Changa replied. "She will lead us to the sheikh."

"How do you know she can do it?" Asif challenged. "She's only a child."

Changa was surprised. "You do not know?"

Zakee seemed to be getting irritated. "Know what?"

Changa checked his mood with a stern glare. "She is the sheikh's daughter."

Asif's shocked look was in stark contrast to Zakee's controlled rage.

Changa grinned. "I see she was wise enough not to reveal her identity to you both."

"How do you know what she says is true?" Zakee demanded.

Again Changa gave Zakee a cross look. "Panya confirmed her words. She is the sheikh's daughter."

"Then she should be dead!" Zakee exclaimed.

Changa had enough. He stepped toward Zakee, his displeasure obvious.

"You sailed with me long enough to know better," he said. "You would punish the innocent for what the guilty have done?"

"This is not about guilt or innocence," Asif argued. "This is about revenge. It is our way."

"So you'll attempt to kill the girl and lose the real prize, her father," Changa said. "It would be the first stupid decision you have made as sultan." Changa shrugged. "It's of no matter anyway. I won't allow it."

"Won't allow it?" Asif charged at Changa, stopping just short of the Bakonga. "You do not give the commands here! If the sultan deems the child to die she will die. I will see to it myself!"

"No, Asif." Zakee pulled Asif away from Changa. "Changa is right. This is not the way. The girl is not guilty and as he said, she can lead us to her father. I've traveled far with him and have seen many lands and people whose customs differ from ours. Our way is not always the best way."

Zakee stood before Changa and nodded in respect. "I apologize. This has been a difficult time for me and my emotions cloud my reason."

Changa placed his hands on his waist. "It doesn't matter what a person thinks or says as long as he does the right thing in the end."

Changa rubbed his chin. "If the sheikh's forces have fallen back this is the best time for Panya and me to be on our way."

The group left the ramparts. Changa found Panya and Ra'naa preparing for the journey and smiled. Panya had apparently learned of the events and come to the same conclusion. There was no need for her to know of the disagreement that nearly foiled their plan. She wore robes of concealment as did Ra'naa. She also covered her hands and face with a dye that changed her skin tone to that of the Yemeni, at least the skin about her face and hands. There was nothing she could do about her facial features; Changa assumed her face veil would complete the disguise. He would be a problem, but he quickly discovered his role when Panya approached him with a heavy looking bundle.

"Here you are, my servant," she said with a broad grin. "You'll make sure our ass is not overburdened."

Changa snarled at her. "Always the servant." He hefted the pack easily onto his shoulders. Ra'naa appeared soon afterwards. Her ragged garments had been replaced for clothing more suitable for their ruse. She smiled at him, though the sadness behind the expression dimmed its effect.

"So what game do we play?" Changa asked.

"Panya is a wealthy matron lending her support to my father," Ra'naa said. "There are many who believe he can grant them immortality because they have seen his warriors rise from the dead. They do not know the truth."

Changa nodded. "How far are we from your village?"

"Three days," Ra'naa said.

"We may not have that long," Changa surmised. "We will have to make it in two days at the most."

He squatted before Ra'naa. "We will have to walk hard and

fast. Panya and I are used to such hardships. I will carry you if I need to."

"Do not worry about me," Ra'naa replied. "I will keep up."

Changa stood. "I believe you will."

Although the sheikh's forces had pulled back, the trio still waited until dusk before slipping from Sana'a. Zakee argued for archers to cover them just in case something went wrong but Changa refused. It would make their departure too suspicious if someone was watching. They struck out south toward Aden, the logical destination for anyone escaping the city. Once they reached the cover of the tree line they altered their route to the west then to the north. They traveled slowly, cautious of any signs that the sheikh was still surrounding the city. To their surprise they discovered not only had the sheikh pulled his army back; he had abandoned the siege completely. Under normal circumstances Changa would have changed plans. He would have immediately returned to the city and announced the enemy's retreat. But this army was not normal. He did not clearly understand the sheikh's intentions but he was sure they were beyond those of men seeking power and wealth.

The terrain was spotted with abandoned camps and smoldering fires.

"They left recently," Panya commented.

"And quickly," Changa added. He paid close attention to the trash piles and fires. "This is not just an army of the dead. The living are among them as well."

"As I told you, there are those who follow my father because they think serving him is the way to immortality," Ra'naa said.

They continued until they were clear of the siege line. The woods thickened as the landscape took on a normal countenance, unmarred by the forces of war. They lost what little light they had as darkness set fully on the hill lands.

"We'll camp for the night," Changa decided.

"No, we must go further," Ra'naa insisted.

"It serves us no purpose to travel in darkness, young one,"

Changa answered. "We will camp and rest. Tomorrow we will push harder."

Changa and Panya set up camp in a thicket of short bushes. Changa made a small fire while Panya organized her herbs and food for the night meal. Ra'naa stood at the camp's edge, staring into the darkness. As Panya neared the fire with her cooking pot Changa pointed at the girl.

"It seems she has lost her patience," he commented.

"She has hope now," Panya replied. "We have given it to her."

"Can you save her father?"

Panya filled the cooking pot halfway with water from her gourd. "I'm not sure. The jinni inside him is powerful. To raise the dead is a draining spell for a normal shaman. This jinni touches a power that is beyond most. Whomever it possesses suffers greatly in return, for normal flesh was not meant to contain such power for such a long period of time. It is difficult enough for us to contain our own souls."

Panya's words worried him. "So what of Kintu's gift? What is it doing to me?"

Panya smiled at Changa, the firelight dancing on her lovely face. "You are an exception, prince of the Kongo. You have the blood of a king which means you are closer to the spirits than most of us. You were created to carry a heavier burden. If you weren't you would have died long ago."

"I have you to thank," Changa replied.

Panya giggled. "I have only aided what was already inside you."

She turned her attention to Ra'naa.

"Come child," she called out. "Our dinner is nearly done."

Ra'naa didn't reply. She continued to stare into the darkness.

Changa stood. A sensation crept up his back as he stared at the girl.

"Ra'naa?"

Ra'naa turned toward them slowly. There was sadness in

her eyes.

"I'm sorry," she said.

She ran into the darkness.

A torrential force slammed into Changa, knocking him onto his back. Panya screamed; Changa attempted to rise but the force pressed him down like a stone on his chest. He strained against the unseen pressure and a familiar feeling formed inside him. Strength rushed through him; he tore himself away from the force in time to see Panya rising into the darkness in the grip of an invisible hand. Fear gripped her face and then she was gone, vanishing into the darkness like an extinguished flame.

Panya's fading scream was usurped by the drumming footfalls coming in Changa's direction. He grabbed Panya's herb bags then entered the night, crouching low to the ground. He did not need to see what he knew approached; the sheikh's men were returning to resume their siege. He wasn't certain if they had seen him at the fire; if so they would be searching for him soon. Going back to the city was out of the question. He would find Panya first before he did anything else.

The footfalls came closer; Changa did not move. Only when he was swarmed by the horde did he leap to his feet. He did not fight them. Instead he ran with them, losing himself in the distorted horde. He traveled with an army of horror, cloaked men with various weapons running alongside the living dead in various stages of decay. Some of the risen carried weapons; some did not for they had no limbs to hold them. Though the live warriors were all men, the deceased were male and female, old and young. Kintu's gift suddenly surged through his body but he dared not take on such a huge horde. He ran with them for one reason. They would attack the city and hopefully they would fail. When they did he would return with them to the sheikh's lair and hopefully find Panya, if she was still alive.

The thought of her death almost turned him away. He should be running the other way, but he would be running blind. The only people that could lead him to the sheikh's lair were his own. He had to follow through to have a chance of seeing her again. This was more than an obligation to a member of his crew, but he knew that long ago. Their time together in the Middle Kingdom had opened emotions that grew with every day, his only respite when he was under Sharmila's spell.

The sentry lights of Sana'a came to view on the dark horizon. Moments later a warning horn blared and the shouts and urgings of men rose over the walls. Changa smiled when he heard Zakee's voice rise over the din. He was on the wall organizing the defenses. Changa fell back as the grotesque army surged ahead. A shower of arrows, invisible in the night, fell upon the attackers and brought them down in scores. There were no cries of pain or exhortation, only grunts and footfalls as the sheikh's men continued their eerie march. Blazing projectiles leaped over the city walls, rising like separate suns then crashing down onto the army. Their burning light illuminated the war zone and revealed the extent of the army. It was a vast group; lacking the fever of a determined foe but moving forward like a relentless flood.

Changa finally spied what he searched for. A second group of men emerged from the darkness bunched in teams and led by cloaked ones carrying torches that glowed with ethereal brightness. They pointed at the fallen men, who were rolled onto leather stretchers. Changa followed the stretcher bearers and their leaders. Though he burned to help Zakee and the others defend the city, a more urgent fire blazed in his heart. He had to find Panya.

The bearers and their masters moved swiftly through the shrubs and trees. Changa found it difficult to keep pace but he managed to keep them in sight. The ground began to slope; Changa entered a valley illuminated by the fires of a vibrant city. Though not as large as Sana'a, it was a city nonetheless that murmured with activity. Other groups approached the town as well, all bearing the dead on stretchers or piled in oxen pulled carts. As he neared the city a rhythmic chant pulsing with the cadence of high pitched drums reached his ears. The flesh salvagers had done what he hoped they would do and Ra'naa never intended to do. They had led him to the lair of the Red Sheikh.

A bonfire blazed, its light streaming though the spindly

figures surrounding it. They swayed to the rhythm, breaking their line periodically to let the body bearers through. Changa was not interested in the ceremony; his purpose was to find Panya. He worked around the ring, searching for the infamous sheikh. If he found him he was sure to find Panya. On the other side of the human barrier the slain warriors were dumped into a narrow lagoon of thick green liquid which bubbled from the heat of the bonfire. The cloaked ones pushed the bodies along with long stained poles, chanting as they passed the body to the next person. By the time the body reached the final acolyte there was movement. The final acolyte, a large brute whose muscles were prominent despite the consuming garb, grasped the body with a wicked hooked staff and pulled the writhing body to the shore. He reached down with a gloved hand and lifted the revived creature from the morbid broth then tossed it to the waiting servants. The result was a person brought back to a life, a grim forfeit for the peace of death.

Changa made a complete circle around the macabre process in frustration. He did not find Panya, nor did he find the Red Sheikh. He retreated into the darkness, desperation stealing his breath and making him pant. It was obvious that magic was at work and there had to be a source to that magic. It was possible the acolytes possessed the power to bring back the dead but it was highly unlikely. They were not the source; whatever or whomever it was had to be nearby.

Changa's patience was rewarded moments later. An acolyte dropped his staff and stumbled from the pool. Anther acolyte took his place; they exchanged words in a language Changa did not recognize. The fatigued acolyte stumbled away and headed into the darkness. Changa made his way to the other side of the pool as fast as possible, catching site of the acolyte before he was lost to the dark. For a long time both men traveled in complete darkness, Changa's senses stretched to the limit to follow a man who apparently knew by heart his destination. A light appeared in the distance, outlining the acolyte and easing Changa's efforts. As the light grew brighter a large building did so as well. It was a fortress, not one of recent construction, but a crude square structure that hinted of a time long lost. A tall, wide, gateless entryway beckoned the acolyte; he quickly disappeared inside. Changa hesitated; studying the flat ramparts to make sure no one guarded the perimeter for intruders like him. The Red Sheikh was apparently confident in himself; there were no guards along the citadel wall. He sprinted across the open ground and into the citadel.

There was a brief moment of darkness and then the light returned, supplied by narrow torches that leaned from the wall in metal braces. The single hallway continued straight into the citadel. Changa held his Damascus tight, his eyes darting from left to right as he followed the footfalls of the acolyte. The footfalls stopped and so did Changa. He crouched and listened.

"Why have you returned?" a deep voice growled.

"My power is spent, Sheikh," the man answered, his fear made real in his trembling soprano.

"Why should I grant my blessing to so weak a vessel? The others still work yet you stand before me begging for more power."

Heavy steps echoed into the hallway. They came closer and Changa tensed his thick muscles, ready to strike like a mamba.

"You are worth more to me carrying a sword than holding my power."

Changa heard the sounds of struggle then a loud snap. The next sound was one too familiar to him. It was the sound of a body falling carelessly to the ground.

"Take him to the lagoon," the deep voiced one said. "He'll serve me better with the others."

The heavy footfalls faded. Changa edged back into the darkness and two acolytes strode by him dragging the body of the hapless man he'd followed into the lair. He would be immersed in the sheikh's concoction, renewed then sent to the walls of Sana'a.

"They all disappoint me," the sheikh said. "As did you."

Changa crept to the end of the corridor. The Red Sheikh sat on a golden throne crowned with a canopy of lapis lazuli bound in silver. The pale man's severe face was barely visible through the glow of the red fabric encircling it and crowning his head with a towering turban. The rest of his body was equally concealed; it was obvious a powerful physical frame pulsed just beneath the crust of fabric. Though the sight of the sheikh moved Changa's emotion, two other visions sparked his anger and stirred the gift he'd been given in Zimbabwe long ago. The child sat beside the sheikh, a sorrowful look on her face. And there was Panya, lying at the sheikh's feet, her clothes ripped and her body still.

"You impressed me with your tricks within the city," the sheikh continued. He waved his hand and spat at her. "Mere tricks from a savage. To think that I wasted my daughter's time to bring you here and watch you die from the weakest of my tortures. Better that I brought your dull witted guardian. His bulk alone might have provided some amusement."

Kintu's gift surged though Changa. Panya stirred at the sheikh's feet and the jinni smiled.

"So you are not dead after all! There still may be some amusement left for me yet."

Panya's eyes cracked open and she stared directly at Changa. The message in them was clear: *go back.*

Changa did not heed it. He charged from the dark corridor, throwing knives in each hand. Ra'naa sprang to her feet, her eyes wide with shock. The Red Sheikh stood slowly, a triumphant smile ruling his face.

Changa was only a few steps into the vast room when he sensed the tebos. He spared little thought for Usenge's assassins; how they came to be with the sheikh did not matter to him. In one swift motion he sent throwing knives at both creatures without taking his eyes off Panya. The blades struck the tebos with such force they toppled backwards as the knives cleaved their skulls simultaneously. Such was the power of Kintu's gift.

The Red Sheikh stumbled back as well, shock and anger distorting his already warped face. The emotion dissipated quickly, replaced by a wide grin. He opened his right hand as Changa charged. A dense smoke rose from his palm, writhing and lengthening until it took the shape of a wide bladed scimitar.

"Come to me, warrior," the sheikh hissed. "Let me triumph

where your master's creatures failed!"

The Red Sheikh jumped, rising into the air like a falcon. He fell on Changa with alacrity; his abnormal descent obviously fueled by his dark powers. Changa checked his attack and jumped forward. He rolled and came to his feet, sword drawn. Panya still lay before him, her eyes reflecting her despair. Changa wanted to go to her but he knew it would be in vain if he did not deal with the sheikh first. He pivoted on the balls of his feet to see the sheikh struggling to free his blade from the stone floor. He ripped it free as Changa advanced.

There was no hesitation between the two, no wary stalking to access each other's skill. They plunged into battle, their swords striking and flashing like a maelstrom. The Red Sheikh's blows were swift and powerful but Changa matched his fury. Fueled by Kintu's gift he was a match for the jinni's power. They danced about the room in a furious blur, their only witnesses cowering from the battle.

Changa knew he could not depend on the spiritual force that enhanced his strength. The jinni's powers were vast, probably far deeper than his temporary powers. He would have to end this fight before he lay on the floor with Panya in a much worse state. He began to slow his pace, barely deflecting the jinni's attacks. His attacks transformed to defense. He backed away, a look of desperation on his once determined face. The jinni smiled, pushing Changa harder, letting his skill wane as he pressed for a killing stroke. Changa fell to his knees, his arms falling to his sides. The Red Sheikh, sensing triumph, gripped his huge blade with both hands and raised it over his head.

"Time to die, little man!" he yelled.

Changa sprang for the opening like a simba. He drove his blade deep into the Red Sheikh's chest, drew it out and stabbed him again. He stabbed the jinni a third time before it realized his ruse. He stumbled back, eyes wide. The scimitar fell from his hands, becoming smoke again before reaching the floor. The jinni ran his hands across his wounds then stared at the blood. When he looked up his face was tight with rage.

"Damned weak vessel!" he cried. He smiled, an expression that unnerved Changa more than his sneers.

The sheikh trembled then fell to the floor. Changa did not savor his victory; he immediately ran to Panya's side.

"Are you hurt?" he said.

"I'll be fine," she replied. "Help me stand. We must be gone quickly. This is not over."

Changa wrapped his arms about Panya and lifted her to her feet.

"What are you talking about? The sheikh is dead."

Panya steadied herself in his arms. "The man whose body he possessed is dead. You cannot kill a jinni. He seeks another host. If he finds one he will return and…"

Changa heard them long before he saw them. Hundreds of voices raised in anger, approaching the temple like a violent wave. He pushed Panya away to arm's length.

"Can you fight?"

Panya took two knives from his belt. "I have no choice, do I?"

"There may be another way out," Changa surmised.

"There is no way out." Ra'naa approached them and Changa raised his sword. He was not one to kill a child, but this young one had almost cost Panya her life.

"Why would a god need to escape his own temple?"

The corridor rumbled with the sound of thousands of footfalls. Changa grasped his sword hilt with both hands as Panya posed with the knives. The sheikh's minions poured into the chamber, some running rapidly while other limped with the broken cadence of the newly resurrected. All had the same burning gaze, confirming what Panya had said. The jinni was not dead, only dispersed. It vacated its host and spread itself into the bodies of its followers hoping to accomplish with numbers what it could not do as one.

Changa had expected to be crushed by a suicidal onslaught. The jinni would not care for the lives he threw into battle, but it seemed the bodies he possessed retained some control over their destinies. They slowed to deal killing blows and Changa and Panya jumped into battle. Changa cut wide swaths with his Damascus, still fueled by his gift. Panya fought like Changa had never seen, spinning and striking with deadly grace as one would expect from a daughter of Oya. Together they held the horde at bay as best they could, ignoring the nicks and cuts accumulating on their bodies. Changa fought relentlessly but Panya faltered, weakened by human limits and her previous ordeal. Changa saw the blade aimed at her chest before she did; he knocked it aside and decapitated the wielder before it reached its mark. He stepped before her as she slumped to the floor exhausted.

Changa continued to battle the horde even as a dark realization surfaced. His gift was failing. Pain crept into his arms. His legs became leaden. A brief surge by the possessed soldiers pushed him back against Panya, but her moan sparked fresh energy into his limbs. He fought back like cornered prey, clearing a wide space. But still they came.

Changa's sight blurred. His motions, while still effective, became almost mechanical; parry, slash, block, stab, dodge, slice, parry, slash… man after man fell to his blades, but they still came. A difference materialized before him. Just one man stood before him, his image indistinct, and a darker vision than the scores he'd slain. Was it the jinni finally in one form, coming to finish him? Changa grinned inside, too tired to raise the corners of his mouth. He did not die easy before. He would not now.

"Changa!" The voice shouting his name was familiar. Was it the jinni trying to distract him with one of his tricks?

"Changa, stop!" the voice said again. Zakee. That's who he sounded like. Changa continued to attack, driving the dark image back.

"Changa stop! You'll kill him!" It was Panya. This was no demon's farce. It was her voice filled with desperation. The sound of her voice cleared his vision and his adversary became clear. A blue robed man, face hidden except for two eyes that stared at him in desperation.

"Tuareg?" he croaked.

The blue man nodded vigorously as he struggled against Changa's blind attack. Changa's arms dropped to his side, his weapons like boulders in his swollen hands. He opened his hands and they clanged against the floor. Changa fell to his knees then fell forward in exhaustion.

The Tuareg caught him then gently laid him onto his back. "Panya?" Changa managed to say.

Hands touched his shoulders, soft yet firm hands, Panya's hands. Her face appeared before him, bruised, bloody, and beautiful. He tried to smile.

"Get him up quickly!" It was Zakee, his voice firm. "We're done here."

Panya disappeared and other hands touched him. Hard, strong hands lifted him onto a litter and he was transported out of the Red Sheikh's chamber. Sunlight forced him to close his eyes; he had apparently fought throughout the night and into the day.

Changa opened his eyes again and gazed across the room. Across the floor Ra'naa hung over her father's body, her sobs reaching his ears. Zakee's men gazed upon her, their sympathetic faces assuring Changa that no harm would come to her. She had done what she did out of love and hope. There was no need to punish the daughter for what a jinni had done. She had suffered enough. Changa winced as he turned his head away. Panya was being carried as well, the two of them surrounded by baharia. They looked at Changa and Panya, the joy in their smiles obvious. The Yemeni soldiers crowded around them as well, their attention bordering on reverence. They approached him one by one, touching his garment gently and whispering words in Yemini. Zakee appeared and smiled.

"Again you excel over all expectations, bwana," he said.

"I would have been grateful not to have the opportunity," Changa complained.

"What are your men saying about me?"

"Changa the demon-slayer," Zakee answer. "It seems you have earned another title."

Changa managed to smile. "I like Changa the living

merchant better."

Zakee grinned. "Rest, Changa. You have earned it."

Changa smiled. "Listen to you giving me orders. You sound like a sultan."

Zakee's face seemed to mature before his eyes.

"I am," he replied.

"Yes, you are," Changa agreed. He closed his eyes and drifted to sleep.

6

THE LOST AND THE FOUND

Changa awoke enveloped in a soft mattress and covered with finely woven cotton sheets. He sat up slowly then realized he was not alone. Looking quickly to his side he smiled. Panya lay beside him, her eyes opening as a playful smile came to her face.

"Good morning," she whispered.

"It is, indeed."

Panya reached up and pulled him down to her. They kissed, Changa savoring the taste of her like sweet fruit after a long journey at sea. And it had been a journey. Not since they left the Middle Kingdom had she let him touch her in such a way.

"So what does this mean?" he asked.

"It means my heart and my head agree, Changa Diop," she replied.

They settled into each other's arms, both too wounded to do much else. There was a light rapping on the door.

"Enter," Changa called out.

Zakee and the Tuareg entered the room. Zakee strode in with a large smile on his face. The Tuareg's eyes reflected his approval.

"So it is finally true!" Zakee blared. "The men can stop whispering."

"No they can't," Changa barked in false anger. "Nothing they think is true until I say so."

Zakee planted his hands on his waist and shook his head. "I would love to leave you two here to enjoy your union, but we must return to Aden. With the Red Sheikh dead my duties lie on the coast."

"We'll be on," Panya assured him.

Zakee looked skeptical. He bowed and turned to leave. The Tuareg lingered for a moment, his eyes saying what he suspected. Changa laughed.

"We will be!" he chuckled.

It was well after noon before the two emerged from their room. Neither were the type to show their desire in public, but both glanced at each other with giddy smiles. By the time they stepped into the courtyard their passions were corralled. Zakee rode with Asif, inspecting the warriors. The Tuareg sat on his horse, holding the reins of Changa's and Panya's mounts. He glared at his companions.

Changa mounted his horse. "So we're a little late. Can you blame me?"

Zakee rode up to them. "We lost half a day, but to see you two together is worth it? Will you marry her in Aden?"

Changa and Panya both looked stunned. Zakee looked back, apparently expecting an answer. The Tuareg's squinting eyes displayed his silent laughter.

"I think we'll ride to Aden," Panya answered.

Zakee looked crestfallen. "It would be an honor if you chose to marry here. My people would be witness to a great event. No expense would be spared."

"Are we leaving or not?" Changa grumbled. He wasn't fully recovered and his tryst with Panya didn't help.

Zakee grinned then nodded at Asif. The Yemini yelled out orders and the warriors fell into place. A small garrison would stay behind to protect the trade routes, but other than those few the army of Sultan Zakee, liberator of Sana'a, was returning to Aden. They rode through the gates and into the hill without fanfare. Most were weary and anxious to get home to their loved ones. The baharia were in no better shape. Changa could see it in their eyes. They were eager to get back on board and follow the winds home.

Toward dusk they had travels ten miles, a good pace for such a hilly landscape. Zakee called a halt and the men broke to set up camp. The provision wagons had been filled with more than enough food to take them back to Aden. Sana'a's residents were grateful and showed it in their donations to the army's commissary.

The largest fire blazed in the presence of Zakee. The new sultan sat surrounded by his old friends and his new subjects, entertained by a friendly competition between the baharia and the Yemini. Baharia drummers played alongside the Yemini as men from both groups danced in their perspective styles. The Yemini obviously thought they were the best dancers, but the baharia's added acrobatics put them to shame.

"Your men are cheating!" Asif complained. "They fly through the air like eagles. That is not dancing!"

"It is in Swahililand," Changa argued. "And my men are the worst dancers. That's why they're sailors. They were sentenced to a life at sea because they didn't deserve to live on land because of their terrible dancing."

Asif studied Changa suspiciously then grinned. Both men laughed.

"You are a good liar, Changa," Asif said. "But you are a better fighter."

"You and your brothers are formidable as well," Changa answered. "We were lucky to have them with us. Their skill with the bow rivals that of the Nubians."

Zakee stood. "It is you we should thank, Changa. You killed the Red Sheikh. Little did I know that a Swahili merchant would be my best teacher."

Zakee then turned his attention to the Tuareg. "And to you, Tuareg. You have become like a brother to me. I look forward to the day your vow of silence is complete and we can converse on profound things."

The sultan's smile widened when he looked at Panya. "If Changa had waited any longer I would have offered you the throne beside me."

Panya diverted her eyes as she smiled. "Always the flatterer, Zakee. You'll find your bride among your people. I'm sure your mother has a few in mind."

Zakee raised his hand and the drumming ceased. Changa looked at him standing regally before everyone as the young sultan swept his eyes over the victorious army.

"I thank you all for your valiant service," Zakee began, his resonant voice carrying throughout the camp. "I know I have been away from you for a long time, but I promise to be a fair and just sultan. I have learned many things on my journeys with Changa, things that will strengthen our country and improve our prosperity."

The first arrow struck Zakee in the chest. The second arrow struck close to the first. Zakee was falling when the third arrow arrived, missing the sultan and boring into the ground.

"Zakee!" Panya screamed.

Changa leaped to his feet and ran to Zakee as everyone surrounded them. Panya was at his side soon afterwards. The Tuareg's attention was elsewhere. He snatched the bow and arrows from an approaching archer, climbed on his horse then galloped away toward the hills. Asif's Turkomen followed.

Panya frantically took off Zakee's robe. To Changa's relief Zakee wore a silk undershirt, the shimmering fabric stained with his blood. It was a trick they learned while among the Mongols. The silk did not break, making the removal of an arrow from a wound easier.

"What is…who would…?" Zakee sputtered.

Panya twisted the arrows free. She brought the tip of each arrow close to her nose. Her shoulders slumped as tears welled in her eyes.

"Poison?" Changa strained to say.

Panya nodded her head. "It's too close to the heart. I can't stop it."

Changa looked at Panya in disbelief. "You have to try!"

Tears rolled down her face. "There's nothing I can do."

Changa grabbed her wrist. "Try, damn it! Try!"

Zakee reached out and touched his hand. Changa looked into the amir's eyes.

"You saved me once, Changa," Zakee whispered. "You cannot save me again. It is Allah's will."

Zakee looked at the both of them, his face seemingly content.

"Laa ilaaha illa-Allah," he whispered. He smiled once again then closed his eyes.

Panya wailed, her head pressed against Zakee's still chest. Changa looked at Zakee's face overcome by weakness. Not since Belay's death had he felt such sadness. He looked up into Asif's tear streaked face as the vizier mumbled. The camp fell silent as every man knelt where they stood and hung their heads. Changa's mourning was interrupted by a sudden realization. He stood then searched the kneeling mourners.

"Where is the Tuareg?" he wondered.

***

The horse struggled over the dune, its breath labored. Foam gathering around its panting mouth but its rider would not relent. The Tuareg jammed his heels into the horse's sides and it snorted in protest. Its pace did not quicken as it crested the dune then stumbled down the opposite side. When it reached the bottom it stopped where it stood, refusing to move any further. The Tuareg dismounted then snatched his weapons from the horse. He raised his scimitar to kill the insolent beast but thought better of it. There would be enough killing when he reached his destination. This would be his last show of mercy for some time.

The Tuareg trudged into what seemed like endless sands with the vigor of a well fed and well rested man. The reality was far from true. Since leaving the Yemini encampment three days ago he had not rested. The riders that accompanied him turned back after the first day. They were mercenaries, and though they fought valiantly during Sana'a's siege they saw no reason to continue a blind pursuit of an assassin they'd never seen. The Tuareg kept his mind focused on the journey before him. He would not allow the image haunting him to appear fully in his mind for if it did he would lose his will to continue.

Zakee was dead. Of that he was certain. He knew the moment the first arrow sank into his friend's chest. The accuracy of the shot could only have been achieved by an assassin, and a very good one at that. The arrow would surely be poisoned. Its position assured a quick death. Not even Panya's potent potions would be able to save him. There was only one thing left to do, and that was seek revenge. The Tuareg would have hesitated, consulting Changa in a silent conversation of the merits of such a journey and the dangers involved. But the Tuareg had been usurped, replaced by a personality buried long ago that emerged to do what a reasonable, pious man could not. The Tuareg had been put aside for the time being. El Sirocco had taken his place.

By daylight the end of the desert beckoned him, a strip of palms and grasses running the length of the horizon. Sirocco was happy to see the oasis, but not for obvious reasons. If he was lucky he would find another mount, a camel preferably, which would speed his pursuit. He marched into the oasis, scattering the women and children who moments ago rested beside the small clear pool. The men closed around him but kept their distance. The Tuareg went directly to the pool then knelt before the water. He lowered his shesh and took a deep drink, his only refreshment since leaving Sana'a. Then he stood and marched toward the camels. The men followed, their nervous hands gripped around the hilts of their meager swords and old spears. They were not fighters but they would fight vigorously to protect their family and their property. It would be a pitiful waste of their lives.

He stopped before the beasts and inspected them. Someone cleared his throat; the Tuareg turned his head to see the face of an old man, his fearful face grizzled with gray hair.

"Sir, we ask that you leave us be." The old man was flanked by two younger men whose faces were more distraught than the elder. It was they who would have to fight if the Tuareg refused and they seemed to sense that their lives hung on his decision. The Tuareg ignored the old man as he continued to inspect the camels. One beast finally caught his eye. It was below his standards but the best of the lot. He approached the beast and grabbed its reins.

"Hey! That's my camel!"

A tall man with broad shoulders and a thick beard emerged from the crowd. He walked up to the Tuareg, his face more worried than confrontational.

"You can't take my camel! What will I ride?"

The Tuareg reached into his robes and extracted a bag. He tossed the bag to the man then walked away with the camel. The man opened the bag.

"Praise to Allah!" he shouted.

The others gathered around him and added their shouts to his. There was more gold in the bag than wealth in the entire oasis. The man could buy three herds of camels.

The Tuareg rode out of the oasis and back into the desert. He rested only when the camel needed. By the next morning he spotted a trail before him. He dismounted and checked the sign. It was two camels and two horses traveling slowly. If he pushed he could overcome them by nightfall. He slowed his pace to stay hidden beyond the horizon. The day passed with agonizing slowness. Sirocco checked and re-checked his weapons. He would be ready when the time came.

The sun finally eased below the western horizon. Sirocco urged his camel forward, riding at a good pace until he could see the glow of a campfire in the distance. He stopped the camel and dismounted. Checking his weapons one more time, he proceeded ahead on foot. Two men sat before the fire, enjoying a late meal. He continued until he was in range then took the bow from his back and loaded it. He fired, the first arrow striking one man in the head. The other man jumped to his feet and tried to flee into the darkness but Sirocco's second arrow struck him in the center of his back. Sirocco walked to the camp.

The first man was dead. The second man crawled toward the camels and horses, occasionally reaching at the arrow in his back. Sirocco ignored him as he searched the camp. A piece of parchment lay before the small fire; he picked it up and realized it was a map. The destination revealed what he suspected. He folded the map and hid it in his robes. A horse neighed and drew his attention. The wounded man was attempting to mount the beast. Sirocco walked to the man, took out his dagger and cut his throat. He then went back to the other man then disrobed him. He was slightly larger but his clothes fit good enough. Sirocco folded his garments and put them into one of the assassins' bags. He then sat before the fire and finished the meal of hard cake and dried lamb. Afterwards he gathered up the camels and horses. He'd killed Zakee's assassins but there was one more death remaining. He knew who he was and he knew exactly where to find him.

He came upon the city at mid-afternoon. It was sooner than he planned but he was satisfied nonetheless. The early arrival gave him time to refresh himself then study the citadel rising over the city, the domicile of Khalid. Zakee's brother played the game well. He welcomed his brother kindly and mourned when Wazeer was slain. He took orders from Zakee without hesitation and fought valiantly against the Red Sheikh and his minions. But there was one detail everyone overlooked. As the Tuareg it was easy for him to miss the sign; as El Sirocco it would have been obvious. With the exception of a few bodyguards, Khalid's main army had remained in his citadel. Even his command to send for his army was a lie. He had sent for his assassins instead. Now with the sultan's army victorious but exhausted he would strike with a fresh army and the fact that the only true heir of the sultan was he.

Sirocco had no trouble wandering the city with his weapons. A mobilization was taking place all around him. Wagons flooded the marketplace as goods were confiscated for the army's provisions. Uniformed soldiers marched from house to house conscripting any man of fighting age and a few who were beyond their warrior years. He stole a pomegranate from a stall and cracked it open for the sweet seeds as turmoil swirled around him. A few of the soldiers looked his way but thought better of it. Sirocco strolled in the general direction of the citadel, following the conscripted herd. They were driven to a short wide building a hundred yards right of the citadel. The soldiers yelled, shoved and kicked the conscripts into a decent line. Five soldiers stood before the entrance of the squat building, handing out spears, swords and shields. A soldier rode by him, staring curiously at him. He lingered for a moment, following Sirocco for some time before spurring his horse to a trot. Sirocco decided to be less conspicuous after the encounter, drifting into the narrow alleys to wait until nightfall. He slept for a time as the rigors of his relentless journey took their toll.

When he awoke he was enveloped in darkness. A thin crescent moon hung over him, assuring a deep darkness throughout the city. He checked his weapons one last time then emerged from the alleyway, takouba in his right hand, scimitar in his left. He strode towards the citadel making no effort to disguise his destination. The citadel gates were open, the ramparts unattended. Khalid was confident. There was no opposition in his home city and nothing to fear from his dead brothers. Like all confident men, he was wrong.

The guards before the gates leaned on their spears, their faces clearly displaying their boredom. Sirocco's approached didn't seem to bother them until they saw his swords drawn. Even then their attention seemed more of annoyance than concern. When they challenged him their lances were still held at ease.

"What do you want?" the burly guard demanded.

Sirocco slit his throat with the scimitar. The other man's eyes went wide then drooped when Sirocco plunged the takouba into his gut. Both men had barely fallen to the ground as he walked into the gates to face the other two interior guards. Their surprised expressions twisted into images of pain as they met the same fate as their brethren. Shouts from the ramparts told him that he'd lost the element of surprise. Sirocco sheathed his swords then ran. He snatched the bow from his back and loaded it with an arrow from the quiver on his waist. Arrows whizzed by him as soldiers gathered on the other side of the courtyard, blocking the entrance to the citadel. Sirocco swept his eyes across the rampart. Three archers fumbled with their bows. He stopped and shot, bringing down one archer with an arrow to his chest. He fell and rolled, avoiding the arrow from his companions then rolled up to his knees. He loaded and fired again and the second archer went down clutching the arrow imbedded in his neck. The third archer ran for cover; Sirocco smiled then turned his attention to the soldiers advancing his way.

"Allahu Akbar!" they shouted in unison as they attacked. Sirocco grinned; Allah would not be with them this night. He whipped out his swords, flinging his baldric away and charged into the mass. Their numbers were their undoing. Sirocco flowed through them, slicing and stabbing. The way before him was clear in moments but another obstacle loomed ahead. The doors to the citadel were closing and the ramparts were filling with archers. He ran at full speed, thankful for the rest he gained earlier. The doors were almost closed as he dived into the narrow gap. A shower of arrows thumped into the doors, a few streaking into the building and impaling the guards running to him. He ran by their bodies, ignoring the shouts of the soldiers pursuing him.

If Khalid's citadel was anything like Zakee's, the royal quarters were located at the topmost floor. Sirocco heard the footfalls of the bodyguards coming to thwart him; he only hoped that Khalid was among them. It would save him from fighting his way up the square stairway. His hopes were not to be; he was met by dozens of black clad warriors, swords drawn and faces covered like his.

He did not hesitate. In fact, he ran faster, meeting the horde before they cleared the stairs. He jumped as high as the tallest man then kicked off the wall, landing behind the men. He continued running up the stairs as if it was level ground. The throne room occupied the third level. Two massive guards brandishing wide scimitars rushed to meet him. Sirocco had no time for swordplay. He brought both men down with arrows to their necks, and then tossed the weapon aside as he invaded the throne room.

Khalid sat on the gilded chair, a look of horror on his face.

"Wait!" he cried. "We can discuss this! It doesn't have to be this way!"

Sirocco brandished his scimitar. He would not soil his takouba with the traitorous brother's blood. Khalid stood and took out his scimitar, wielding it with shaking hands. Sirocco feinted; Khalid cried out as he attacked. Sirocco ducked his wild swing and kicked Khalid in the stomach. Khalid doubled over, dropping his blade. Sirocco pushed Khalid to his knees and with one clean stroke severed his head from his body. He kicked Khalid's body over then took his jambiya. Reaching into his robes, he took out a leather bag as he walked over to Khalid's head. He grabbed it by the hair and jammed it into the bag.

A collective gasp drew his attention to the throne room entrance. Khalid's bodyguards and soldiers stared at his body with various expressions of shock and disbelief. This was the weakest link in his plan. What happened next would be based purely on emotion. If they loved the man dead before them they would seek revenge; if they only served the man they would do nothing. It was time to find out which was true.

He walked directly toward them. They looked at him as he came closer, some weapons raised, others lowered. They parted, opening a way for him. Sirocco walked through the eerie gauntlet, his hard eyes focused on the way before him. It seemed to take an eternity to descend the stairs, walk through the grand foyer, and exit the citadel. Others were gathered outside, their eyes transfixed on him as he continued his march. He went directly to Khalid's stables and chose a fine camel. He saddled the beast, mounted it then continued his departure. No one approached him and no one threatened him. They were leaving this between the royals. Sirocco surmised that no matter who ruled Yemen their lot would not change.

As he rode through the gates a solitary wail broke the strange silence. Sirocco did not care who emitted such a mournful sound. His mission was done; revenge was complete. He rode into the darkness and the desert not with satisfaction but with remorse. Zakee was still dead, but at least the man who killed him would not take his place. Sirocco's task complete, he returned to his place, releasing the Tuareg. The Tuareg disappeared into the dark horizon, his heart sorrowful, yet satisfied. Zakee's death was avenged.

7

HOMEWARD BOUND

Zakee's funeral was a modest affair as was custom. Asif prepared his body for burial as soon as Panya declared him dead. They rushed to Aden to deliver the news to his mother and sisters who immediately broke tradition by mourning not only his death, but the death of Wazeer. Zakee's mother could not be consoled; she locked herself away and refused all company, even that of her daughters. Khadeejah step into her place, making the arrangements for the procession and funeral. When Changa first met Zakee's oldest sister he had his suspicions, especially when he discovered her relationship with Asif. But his time with Asif convinced him that the vizier's emotions were sincere. As he watched Khadeejah go about her duties while controlling her emotions he concluded that her intentions were honest as well.

Changa and his crew retired to their dhows soon after Zakee was laid to rest. There they mourned their lost comrade their way. The baharia cried openly, especially those of the *Kazuri* who the young Yemeni had befriended and eventually commanded. Mikaili took to private counsel, retreating to the *Sendibada*'s stern and uttering prayers as he clutched his cross. For Changa it was a complex thing. Only two other times in his life had he lost loved ones; once when he was torn from his family as a boy and again when Belay died.

Panya came to his side and clutched his arm. He slipped it around her shoulders and pulled her close.

"I will miss him so much," she said. "He brought joy to these dhows."

Changa smiled as he remembered Zakee's exuberance.

"That he did." He looked at Aden, the bustling harbor city climbing into the hills. He slammed his fist against the railing.

"I should have never brought him home! We could have stopped in another port and took on supplies then headed to

Mogadishu."

"You know this is what he wanted," Panya replied. "He wanted to come home, Changa, and he did. You should be happy that you were able to help him."

"Help him die!" Changa barked.

"It was his fate," Panya consoled. "It was chance that we saved him before. If we had not needed provisions Zakee would have died alone and desecrated. Instead he leaves a short but powerful legacy. He became a sultan and he defended his people from the Red Sheikh. He will be remembered with honor. It was a good life."

Changa was about to reply when he noticed a camel and dark clad rider in the distance. He pointed to them, drawing Panya's attention.

"The Tuareg returns," he said.

Changa dispatched a boat that met the Tuareg on the shore. They returned quickly; the Tuareg trudged to Changa, his eyes weary and sad. He dropped a leather bag at Changa's feet then reached into his cloak and extracted a jeweled jambiya.

Changa looked at the bag, his nose crinkling from the stench. He took the jambiya from his friend then placed a welcoming hand on his shoulder.

"We mourn in our own way," Changa said.

He felt the Tuareg tremble before he nodded. Changa glanced at the bag.

"Khalid?"

The Tuareg nodded again, the glint of satisfaction in his eyes.

"Rest a moment, friend. It seems we must visit the citadel."

Changa, Panya, and the Tuareg boarded a boat and set out for the citadel. Mikaili refused to go. They rode to the palace and were quickly escorted inside with their morbid package. Khadeejah, Asif, and Zakee's mother sat before them. The look on Khadeejah's face let Changa know that she anticipated their visit.

"You asked for a council," she said. "What is it that you

wish to discuss?"

"It seems you have some decisions to make," Changa replied. He nodded to the Tuareg who stepped forward with the leather bag and the jambiya.

"No, no!" Zakee's mother wailed. She jumped from her chair and fled the room, Zakee's sisters close behind. Only Khadeejah and Asif remained.

"I take it this is Khalid's jambiya...and his head," Khadeejah said. There was no sorrow in her expression or voice.

"It is," Changa replied. "It seems that you are now sultana."

Khadeejah's eyes closed as she lifted her hand to hold her forehead.

"I cannot think of this," she said. "This is not happening."

Changa shrugged his shoulders. "It is what it is. We all do what we must. Asif is a capable leader and I'm sure he'll be eager to assist you."

Asif squirmed in his seat. "I will serve the Basheer family in any way they require."

Changa smirked. "I'm sure you will. Something tells me you already have."

Khadeejah glared at Changa for a moment then gave him a sly smile. Changa smiled back.

"What of you, Changa Diop? You stood by my brother as a true friend and you saved us from the sheikh. You and you crew are encouraged to stay and help us."

"Thank you for the invitation, but it is time for us to go," he answered. "There is much work for you to do but you don't need our help. We are but a handful of men. Our absence will not be noticed."

Khadeejah left her seat. She approached the Tuareg first, nodding to the silent warrior.

"He thought of you as an uncle, and I know you loved him, too."

The Tuareg's eyes glistened. He nodded and turned away.

Khadeejah then approached Panya.

"When I first met you I was suspicious. You have Bahati's beauty, but your heart is pure and my brother cared deeply for you. I will always think of you as a sister."

The women embraced. Khadeejah then stood before Changa.

"Zakee considered you a second father," she said. "During our brief reunion he spoke of you constantly, talking of how much he learned from you. He said if he was blessed to become a great sultan it would be because of your lessons and guidance. Thank you for bringing him back to us."

Khadeejah hugged Changa. The burly Bakonga returned the gesture while fighting to hold back his own tears.

Khadeejah released him and returned to her chair. "Travel safe, my friends. Allah keep you safe. Remember that no matter where you go, you always have a safe harbor in Aden."

***

Changa watched from the stern as Aden diminished into the distance. He stood alone; the Tuareg chose to stand at the bow, while Panya busied herself below deck. Mikaili occupied the wheel, still refusing to speak. It had been a long safari. The hulls of his ships held the treasures of trade, yet at that moment Changa's heart was empty. He had his own homecoming before him, one that could end like Zakee's. He shook his head to rid himself of the thought. He looked at his waist to the parting gift from Khadeejah, Zakee's jambiya. He touched the hilt and smiled.

"Goodbye, my friend," he whispered. "Our lives will be less bright without you."

Changa took a final look at Aden. He turned away and ambled to Mikaili.

"Where to?" Mikaili asked.

"Mogadishu," Changa replied.

Changa looked over his shoulder one last time then set his eyes on the distant horizon.

KITABU CHE SITA:
(BOOK SIX)
PROTECTOR OF THE COVENANT

1

THE NEW MASTER

The creature glided across the expansive sand, its appetite wetted by the nearness of what it sought. Time meant nothing to the wandering spirit; its purpose was its only reason for being. For countless months it had roamed the continent, Usenge's command echoed repeatedly in its simple thoughts, the rhythm of the words fueling its every action.

Find the son of Mfumu. Kill the son of Mfumu.

The tebo halted, hovering over the barren sand. Something stirred beneath it, a presence more compelling than its purpose. Its master's chant faded until it vanished, replaced by a simple command that filled its consciousness and compelled it to action.

Come.

The tebo plunged into the earth, passing though the layers of sand and clay as easily as it glided through air. Dense darkness enveloped it for a time then the spirit emerged into a vast cavern. Below it a massive river flowed, its shadowy banks lined by luminous plants. The tebo hovered, seeking the voice that commanded it into the depths.

Follow the river.

The tebo obeyed, following the meandering waterway until it abruptly plunged into misty blackness. The spirit descended through the mist clouds to a large lake. On the opposite side of the lake was a stone structure similar to those of the northlands the creature had scoured in search of Mfumu's son. It glided quickly across the still water then stopped before the towering stone door.

Enter.

The tebo passed through the doors and entered a massive mausoleum. Hundreds of skeletons garbed in decaying leather armor and shallow metal helmets lined a path of ivory and gold that originated at the base of the thick doors and ended at a dais in the center of the room. The dais was surrounded by marble thrones, each holding a skeleton draped in jewelry. Some were the size of adults, while others were much smaller. More skeletons languished at the base of the thrones, most human but many of animal origin.

The scene meant nothing to the tebo. It reached its destination, a tomb which held the wealth of a thousand empires imbedded into its sides. The light illuminating the crypt emanated from a large sphere embedded at the head of the tomb. The light irritated the tebo, forcing it to drift away. Before it could leave the command gripped it again.

Open.

The tebo returned then surrounded the tomb. The light was defiant, flaring vigorously and pushing at the tebo's mystical form but the spirit was persistent. Finally the light relented, sputtering into nothing. The tebo condensed, becoming tangible as it concentrated its strength on the lid of the tomb. The mausoleum echoed with the sound of stone sliding against stone as the tebo opened the tomb. As the lid crashed onto the marble a searing brightness enveloped the spirit. Images formed in its mind, visions of a long forgotten kingdom which ruled over a land of grass where sand now held sway. The vision of a man formed as well, not the masked countenance of the tebo's original master, but the stern, handsome face carved in ebony with eyes lit with a sorcerer's essence. The tebo found its essence diminished by this new spirit. It fought back instinctively but was no match for this surge. Feelings swelled the memories; whatever lay in the tomb had not died but rested, waiting for the time it could emerge again. It had been many years, thousands, it suspected, but now it was free. The tebo watched the transformation without emotion. This new master had usurped but not destroyed it. It was needed to sustain the new master, so it was still useful. The purpose which had been dulled emerged again and the tebo embedded its duty onto the new master's thoughts. Though it was no longer in control, the purpose still existed. The son of Mfumu would die.

2

Unfinished Business

Eight dhows sped across the Arabian Sea, their sails full with the monsoon winds. Baharia busied themselves on the decks, administering the constant care needed for a ship at sea. It had been a long safari, a journey filled with adventure, danger and loss. Now they were on their way home, eager for their families and familiar sights. It was occasion for good spirits, but a pall hung over them all. The loss of a crewmember was never taken lightly among these baharia, but the loss of a special member weighed deeper.

Changa sat in his cabin, his eyes wide with displeasure as Mikaili stood opposite him. The tall Ethiopian looked back at him just as intensely but without his normal sarcasm. He seemed solemn, almost melancholy, which gave weight to the words he'd just uttered. Still Changa refused to believe him.

"You're not serious," Changa said.

"I am," Mikaili replied. "It's time."

Changa smirked. "You said that before, I believe. It was before you came to work for me."

Mikaili pulled up a stool and sat. "When I accepted your offer I realized the desire still burned inside me. In the beginning it was exactly like I remembered. You can't imagine how happy I was. But now…"

Changa leaned back into his chair. "This is about Zakee."

Mikaili touched his cross. "I'm tired, Changa. Tired of the sea; tired of losing friends. It's time I answered my calling."

Changa raised his hands. "So what do I do? You leave and I have no navigator."

"You have Nafari," Mikaili answered. "He's worked beside me since we sailed from the Middle Kingdom."

"Nafari is competent but he is not as good as you."

"Changa, what do you need me for?" Mikaili asked. "We sail for Mogadishu, then Pemba and finally Sofala. Nafari is skilled enough to take you this far. You could navigate these waters. Besides, what are your plans beyond Sofala? Whatever they are I don't think they involved a navigator."

Mikaili was correct. Once they reached Sofala Changa's plans would shift to returning to his homeland. The thought made him nervous; that would mean a confrontation with Usenge and the tebos. But it was what he planned since the day he fled his homeland.

Changa shifted in his seat. "What if I change my mind? What if I decide to make another safari to the Middle Kingdom? I do have a debt to collect from the emperor."

"I will not change my mind, Changa," Mikaili looked at Changa then looked away. "My days on the sea are over."

"It would have been more convenient if you had come to this decision in Aden. We could have sailed to Djibouti and be done with it!" Changa barked.

"This was not an easy decision," Mikaili said softly. "It's hard to leave your family."

He stood and hurried from Changa's cabin. Changa stared at the stool, too stunned to be upset. He was still staring at the stool when Panya entered his cabin.

"What's wrong?" she asked. "Mikaili seemed upset."

"Mikaili's always upset," Changa responded.

"Not like this. Changa, tell me what's the matter."

"Mikaili is leaving us. He plans to take up the priesthood."

Panya slumped onto the stool. "Really?"

"So he says."

Panya nodded thoughtfully. "It is the right thing for him to do."

A nervous pain shot through Changa's gut. "What do you mean?"

"We are going home, Changa," she replied. "You have no more need of him."

"I know, but still…"

Panya reached out and he took her hand. Whatever doubt

that existed between them disappeared after Yemen. They were together now, but her statement made him nervous.

"You are not concerned about losing Mikaili's services," she explained. "You are sad about losing another brother."

They were silent for a moment as they both recalled Zakee's death.

"It has been a long safari," Changa said. "We have become…"

"A family," Panya finished.

"Yes, a family."

Panya stood and came to him, sitting in his lap then wrapping her arms around his shoulders.

"When Zakee died I realized how close we all were," she said. "I also realized how much I cared for you."

Changa wrapped his arms around her waist and pulled her tight.

"I have few memories of my family, and the last were not good," he said. "Belay considered me a son, but his true sons made sure that feeling would not be complete from me."

"Mikaili is an old man and the sea is a hard life," Panya said. "It's time for him to go home and rest. Don't make him feel bad about it."

Changa didn't respond. He let Panya go and she stood. She walked to the cabin door then looked back at him.

"It's time for him to go home, Changa. It's time for all of us."

Mogadishu appeared over the horizon with the rising sun, the usually busy shores quiet at such an early time. Changa appeared on the deck and went directly to the helm. Mikaili and Nafari stood side by side, the young bahari steering the dhow as Mikaili whispered instructions to him.

"Why don't you speak plainly?" Changa admonished. "He could hear you better."

Mikaili scowled. "Yes, but then he would not listen. You yell at them all the time and does it do any good? No!"

Changa fought against the smile attempting to grace his face and lost. Mikaili was a much better curmudgeon than he. Oddly, he would miss that.

"Mikaili, come with me," Changa asked.

Mikaili's eyes widen. "Can't you see I'm busy?"

"Mikaili, please," Changa insisted.

Mikaili clambered down the steps to Changa.

"What is it?"

"Follow me. We have things to discuss."

Mikaili frowned. "What do we need…?"

Changa raised his hand, silencing him.

"No more of your attitude, not now. Just follow me."

The two men descended into the cargo hold. The wealth of dozens of nations glistened around them; Chinese porcelain, Ceylonese jewels, Indonesian spices, and Hindi gold. Changa sat on a jeweled chest and Mikaili sat beside him.

"As you know I'll split the cargo with everyone once we reach Sofala," Changa said. "But since you're leaving us early you'll receive your portion now."

Changa stood and gestured at the chest. "This is your portion."

Mikaili rolled his eyes upward and let out a breath.

"God has a sense of humor," he said. "I spend most of my life sailing the seas as a servant or a low paid navigator, and now that I commit myself to the priesthood I'm offered a treasure. Changa, you are the devil."

"No, I'm a friend trying to help another friend. If you cannot use this maybe your brethren can. You can use it to buy supplies for your church and help those who need it. That is what you priests do, isn't it?"

Mikaili rubbed his chin. "This would help. I think I will accept my portion, Changa. Thank you."

Changa grabbed Mikaili and wrapped him into a big hug.

"Thank you, Mikaili. You took us to the other side of the world and brought us back."

Mikaili stepped away, a genuine smile on his face.

"You are a man destined for greatness, Changa. I knew it the first time I saw you and you have proven it with every challenge we've face. God is on your side. Who am I to refuse His blessing?"

Changa frowned. "I see the priest in you is beginning to assert itself. Come, let's get back on deck before Nafari runs us aground."

The dhows sailed close to the beach. Changa took a long look at the Mogadishu shoreline and felt a tinge of happiness despite his grim past in the city. He was closer to home than he had been in months and it was hard to hide his joy. Panya and the Tuareg met them on deck.

"So what are our plans for this city?" Panya asked.

"Not much," Changa replied. "We refresh provisions and are on our way. Our cargo is meant for further south."

"Come with me," Mikaili blurted.

Changa looked at him puzzled. "What?"

"Come with me to my home," he said again. "I would like you all to be with me when I'm ordained. It would be an honor."

"That's a wonderful idea!" Panya exclaimed. The Tuareg's eyes brightened as he looked at Changa. Changa had to admit the suggestion was appealing.

"What of our cargo?" Changa asked. "Mogadishu is a city of holy men, but not honest men."

"You said you had no intentions of trading here, so there is no need for oversight," Panya answered. "You know we don't have to worry about our brothers and Nafari is a capable leader. Besides, the men won't cross you. They know better."

Mikaili took on his disgruntled façade. "I'll need your protection as well. You saddled an old man with a king's wealth and expect me to travel though the countryside alone?"

Changa grinned. "So the truth comes out."

"I'm a practical man," Mikaili said. "Besides that reason is more likely to appeal to you than pure emotion."

"I'll go ashore and secure mooring for the dhows," Changa said. "On your suggestion I'll leave Nafari in charge, but if he fails you'll all suffer his fate. Understand?"

Changa's threat barely blemished the smiles on everyone's face. They all scrambled off to prepare for the journey. Changa finally smiled. It would be good to take a journey just for the sake of traveling. Spending some time away would help him clear his thoughts and plan his next moves once he reached Sofala.

Changa and the Tuareg took a boat to shore. The two men stared are the city with solemn faces.

"Many memories here," Changa commented.

The Tuareg nodded, his eyes unblinking.

"I guess some good came of it," Changa shrugged. "This is where I met Belay, and you."

He patted the Tuareg's shoulder and the mysterious man turned to look at him. They said nothing else, each caught up in their own thoughts. When they reached the shore they found the dock master and secured space for his dhows. Changa cringed at the price despite the fact that he could easily afford it.

The duo was working their way through the narrow streets to secure provisions when a familiar voice called out.

"Mbogo!"

Changa closed his eyes and let out a slow breath. It was inevitable that he would meet someone from his past. He had hoped it would be a person that he shared pleasant memories although he made very few of those in the city of his slavery. The man calling out to him was a mixture of good and bad, but one who could not be ignored.

Changa turned to face Bwana Kabili. The old merchant was flanked by two Nuba guards, tall, slender, grim faced men carrying short swords and long spears. Time had been gentle to Kabili; the only sign of the passing years was his graying beard. He approached Changa with arms extended and the men hugged.

"It's been a long time, my friend," Kabili said. "A very long time."

"Yes it has," Changa replied politely. "I see Allah has been kind to you."

"And to you," Kabili answered. He looked past Changa to

the Tuareg.

"I see he still accompanies you."

Changa nodded. "He is with me as a free man of his own choosing. We have become brothers."

Kabili pulled at his beard. "He still doesn't speak."

"It is his vow," Changa answered.

"Where are you headed?" Kabili asked.

"Off to secure provisions. We are taking a journey to the interior."

"I will walk with you," Kabili said. "It's been a while since you've been to Mogadishu. You will need my assistance."

Changa, Kabili, and the Tuareg walked abreast of each other, the Nuba guards close behind. Changa waited for Kabili to state the real reason he wished to accompany him.

"You know, Changa, my store rooms have suffered greatly over the years," he began.

"Is that so?" Changa shrugged. "Our profession is a fickle one."

"That it is," Kabili agreed. "It seems your absence has been the cause of my suffering. Mine and others."

Changa and the Tuareg stole glances at each other. Changa remained relaxed; the Tuareg's hands found the hilts of his swords.

"I make decisions for the best interest of my business, Kabili, as do you," Changa said.

"I understand," Kabili agreed. "But there is one difference between you and me, Changa. I'm Swahili. You are not."

Changa checked his anger. Kabili's statement was an insult which caught him off guard. It shouldn't have, for he had been warned before his voyage by Mulefu that the Swahili would not be pleased with him bypassing the northern ports. Kabili had been sent to deliver the message.

"When you came to me years ago I accepted you against everyone's protest," Kabili said.

"Don't try to make me believe you had a choice," Changa shot back. "You needed me for the ivory only I could deliver.

Rejecting my trade meant finding another supplier."

Kabili smiled. "That is true. Still, I could have said no. But I didn't. Belay's sons still speak against you and they have more than a small influence among the Swahili, especially in Mombasa. They are not the traders their father was, but they still benefit from his status."

"So what do you want?" Changa asked. He was tired of Kabili's threatening banter. In the end the Swahili were traders. Everything had a price.

"You have eight dhows," Kabili answered. "I think the cargo of three of them would be enough to pay for my support."

"Impossible," Changa answered.

"It is my only offer," Kabili replied.

"Then there is nothing left for us to talk about," Changa said.

The Tuareg extracted his swords and turned toward the Nuba guards. The Nuba halted, lowering their spears. A woman screamed and the streets emptied as people ran to escape the violence about to occur.

Kabili raised his hand. "I did not come to fight you, Changa. I'm well aware how such a confrontation would end. No cargo is worth my life."

He passed by Changa and the Tuareg then stood between his guards.

"I'm disappointed in your decision. I think you should know that no Swahili house will accept your cargo. I hope your friends in Sofala can absorb all this wealth. They will be your only market."

Kabili bowed then turned his back on Changa. His guards glared at the Tuareg then followed.

Changa looked at the Tuareg and shrugged. "It's as I thought it would be."

The Tuareg's eyes questioned him and Changa shrugged again. "I did not sail across the world to trade once I returned. Once we return to Sofala Kabili and his friends will no longer need to worry about me or my intentions."

The Tuareg shot Changa a questioning look and Changa looked away. No one knew of his plan to return to Bakongo, not even his constant companion. He did not know if the Tuareg would accompany him but he knew that without him his task would be much more difficult.

"I will tell all in time, my friend," Changa assured him. "Please be patient."

Kabili's threat was quickly forgotten and Changa and the Tuareg gathered provisions for the safari. They returned to the shore with twelve donkeys loaded with supplies and five workers to handle the donkeys and other duties on the road. Mikaili and Panya waited for them at the dhows.

"We'll be leaving for Djibouti immediately," Changa said.

"What's the hurry?" Panya asked.

"It seems we are not welcomed in Mogadishu," he answered. "Our Swahili friends are not happy about our safari east. They refuse to trade with us."

"Does that include Sofala?" Mikaili asked.

"I don't know. I guess we'll find out when we arrive. For now we won't worry about it. We'll load our supplies and sail on. Mogadishu has never been a good city for me. There's no reason that should change now."

The Tuareg nodded in agreement. They both shared bitter memories of the city, so there was no remorse in either of them about leaving so soon. The baharia were another matter.

"What about the men?" Nasiri asked. "We have been long at sea. We were expecting some rest."

Changa smiled. "I know, Nasiri. We'll just be a few more weeks. Besides, I think you can enjoy yourselves much better in Djibouti."

A knowing grin passed among the men. Panya looked at them all and rolled her eyes.

"Djibouti is a foul place," she hissed.

"Yes it is, but it's closer to Axum and we can trade there with no worries from the Swahili."

Panya folded her arms across her chest and shrugged.

The prospect of spending their free time in Djibouti infused the baharia with energy. The donkeys were unloaded quickly, the cargo rowed out to the dhows in small boats. A dead calm lingered over the harbor, delaying their departure. Changa spent time on the deck with the men, helping the men with repairs and maintenance. He was helping with the bulwark when he noticed the gathering on the shore. For one not trained for danger the commotion would have gone unnoticed but to Changa's keen eye there was definitely something amiss. Men draped in cloaks arrived at the beach in groups of three or in duos, lingering among the workers. They made conversation, giving slight nods to other groups as they arrived then cutting glances at the ships in the harbor. Changa ceased working and concentrated on the gathering. He realized after a time the glances weren't random. They were looking at his dhows.

"Tuareg!" he called out. His silent companion came to him almost immediately. His concerned eyes let Changa know that he wasn't the only one who noticed the gathering.

"Take a few men below for the crossbows," Changa whispered. "Prepare the cannons as well. Signal the other dhows and have them prepare as well. I think a storm is brewing."

The Tuareg had barely set out to follow Changa's orders when a distinct voice echoed over the harbor. It was call to prayer; the imams had done so a few hours ago. Another group of men rushed the shore in pairs, carrying heavy gourds that sloshed some type of liquid over the rim. As they sat the gourds on the sand other hurried to the gourds with lit torches.

"Sound the drums!" Changa shouted. "Raise the anchor and man the oars!"

The *Kazuri* sprang to life; the signal drummer rapped out a quick rhythm to alert the other dhows.

The mysterious men threw there cloaks aside, revealing their identities. Changa's face dropped in dread. They were Nuba archers, men whose unmatched skill with the bow stretched back for centuries. They ran to the burning gourds then dipped their cotton swaddled arrows into the fire. They trotted to the shoreline then formed ranks. The baharia turned to the dhow's deck armed with crossbows and led by the Tuareg. They managed to get off a volley of bolts before the Nuba but the shoreline was beyond their range. The *Kazuri*, Changa's main fighting ship, fired its cannon but could not reach the shore as well.

"Get those damn oars in the water!" Changa shouted, desperation clear in his voice.

The Nuba loaded their bows in unison. One of the bowmen, a man only distinguishable by a golden cross hanging on his neck, yelled out an order and the Nuba released their flaming arrows. The lethal downpour easily traveled the distance between shore and ship, ripping through the sails of all three dhows. They were lucky; the Nuba were finding their range. The second volley would be more deadly.

"Take us closer!" Changa shouted. If he could get the *Kazuri* closer they could bombard the shore and scatter the archers. It would give the other dhows time to escape the harbor.

"Tuareg! Get the men prepared for fires!"

Changa waited to see the blue robed man set about his task but he did not appear. Changa ran to the opposite end of the ship and still saw no sign of the Tuareg. He hurried below deck to the cannons and then the oars. Still there was no sign of him.

When Changa returned to the deck Panya waited for him. The look on her face did nothing to ease his mood.

"Changa, look," she said.

Panya pointed toward the shore. Changa grimaced.

"Don't tell me the obvious, woman," he snapped.

"No Changa, look!"

Changa scanned the shore then saw what Panya observed. The Tuareg rose from the water, takouba and scimitar drawn. The Nuba were so busy preparing for their next volley they did not see his attack until he was among them, slicing and stabbing with brutal efficiency. Changa ran to the edge of the dhow and climbed the bulwark. Panya grabbed his shirt and pulled him back down.

"What are you doing?" she shouted.

"I'm going to help him!" Changa shouted back.

The Tuareg's assault disrupted the Nuba barrage but did not stop it. Another volley of flaming arrows soared toward Changa's fleet. Changa saw Panya's eyes widen just before she dove for the deck. He turned and a searing pain tore through his chest. Heat burned at his back as he fell onto the deck. Baharia ran around him, yelling as they fought the numerous fires trying to ignite the ship. Cannons barked and the deck shook beneath him, causing him to wince in pain.

"Get this damn dhow moving!" Mikaili shouted. Changa tried to protest but weakness stifled his voice.

"The winds are finally with us!" Nasiri exclaimed. "Drop sails! Oarsmen, double the pace."

Changa gritted his teeth and sat up. The *Kazuri* baharia whirled about him, fighting fires, working the sails and cursing at the Nuba archers while cheering the Tuareg's efforts. He fought to gather his feet under him but Panya's face appeared. She pushed him back down.

"No," she said sternly. "We are leaving."

"Can't…leave," Changa whispered. "Tuareg…"

Panya looked away for just a moment. "He knew what he was doing, Changa. He's giving us time."

"But he'll die!" Changa tried to rise again.

"No, Changa!" This time Panya held him down, her hands on his shoulders.

"If we go back now we lose everything and everyone. We have to leave."

"But…" Changa closed his eyes to gather strength to protest. Panya shushed him.

"You saved his life," she said. "Now he is saving ours."

Panya suddenly lay over him as another volley of Nuba arrows struck the ship. Changa burned inside, angry that he should be so helpless at such a dire time. There was a chance the Tuareg would live, but it was a slim chance at the most. As he let consciousness slip away, he became certain of one thing. For as long as he lived, he would hate Mogadishu.

3

ANTOTH RISES

Antoth, First of the First, Master of the Realm between Rivers, expected to rise from death in the presence of the gods. He anticipated a gauntlet of gold columns leading to a massive throne on which Mem, God of Gods sat, his perfect smile beckoning him forward. Standing between the columns would be his ancestors, honored men of strength and valor, each one singing his praises as they read from the papyrus scrolls interred with him during his secret burial by his priests. At the end of his solitary procession he would kneel then look up into the perfect onyx face of Mem. Mem would smile then touch his head with his Staff of Truth.

"Well done, First of First," Mem would say. "Take your place among The Honored."

Instead Antoth looked into the gloom that was the belly of his mausoleum. His decayed hands grasped the dusted wood on his mock throne as he gazed at the remnants of his royal house. The bones of his servants sprawled against the walls; those of his wives and concubines littered the steps leading to his seat. A grim thought emerged in his mind. Despite his conquests, his achievements and his sacrifices to them, the gods had not accepted him among their own.

His mind blurred as the essence within him struggled to assert itself. It was a weak thing, the product of a shaman whose current power paled when compared to Antoth's former glory. But a man who starves for life has few choices. The gods rejected him, leaving him to rot for eternity in his tomb. He was Antoth. He would not accept such a fate.

Because he was Antoth, he was also prepared. Trust no one or no thing, even the gods, he would always say. He suppressed the pathetic protests of the spirit and rose from his throne. A weak glow came to his damaged eyes and he scanned his crypt, finally laying sight on the object he sought. He took a step and tumbled to the marble floor, sprawled among the bones of his household. He regained his composure and instinctively scanned the tomb. A dry cackle seeped from his throat. In life, such a mishap would have revealed a flaw in a man who was supposed to be perfect. He would have immediately killed anyone who observed his clumsiness. But accidents among the dead are not seen, thus he enjoyed the humor of the moment.

He stood then shuffled to the collection of gilded chests bordered by the remains of his treasure guards. His eyes centered on a small jade box resting atop a larger golden container. It was modest compared to the others, but when he touched it the room filled with a green tinted glow. Antoth struggled to remember the incantation, his thoughts hampered by millennia of sleep. Finally the words came to him and he whispered. The glow increased and the box opened. Inside, cradled on a pillow of cotton filled silk, lay a small necklace. A black disk hung from a thin golden chain, a disk dark yet emitting a certain light of its own, and an illumination visible only to Antoth's eyes. He lifted the necklace from its bed then absently dropped the box. Placing the necklace around his neck he felt a surge of energy ripple through him. He looked at his limbs, smiling as the grey husk that he was transformed into taut black skin which barely contained the powerful muscles beneath it. The brightness from his eyes increased, expanding across the crypt. The struggling soul within ceased its protests, succumbing to the ancient force that coursed through him.

But it was not enough. He needed more sustenance for what he envisioned. If the gods would not accept him, he would create his own paradise. He'd come so close before time robbed his body. At the moment of death, he saw the truth of immortality. It was a simple thing, really, at least for someone with his skills. His eyes widened and he laughed again. He now understood why the gods had not accepted him. The revelation was almost absurd, but he could see no other reason. Mem, God of Gods, was afraid of him.

Antoth sat in the center of his tomb and closed his eyes. He reached out through the blanket of sand, probing for other objects similar to the one about his neck. His search was incomplete.

Some remained where they had been secreted, while others were missing. Anger flashed through his mind; his false tombs had apparently been desecrated, the spells meant to protect them long spent. He tried to imagine how long he'd been deceased but quickly abandoned the thought. It did not matter now. What mattered was his resurrection.

He would have to go to the discs for he was too weak to summon them. He raised his head and scanned his illuminated eyes across the tomb until he found the entrance. He lifted his left hand, opening the sealed door before he reached it. Sand flowed in like water, rushing over the tomb floor and covering the remnants of his reign. The sand was up to his waist before it ceased but its weight did nothing to deter him. He waded through the granules to the granite steps then climbed slowly from the tomb. Emerging into darkness, he gazed into a sky that was as unfamiliar to him as the barren landscape surrounding him. It was then he noticed it. A source beckoned from the east, a cache of power so intense it brightened the spiritual plane like the sun. His other orbs paled in its intensity. This was the type of power he needed. With it inside him he could subjugate whatever men inhabited this familiar yet different land and build a new empire greater than that of the ancestors.

He was about to gather his other gems when pain bolted through his skull. He fell to his knees clutching his misshapen head. An image appeared, the face of a man he did not recognize but whose visage stirred feelings of intense hatred inside him.

"The son of Mfumu," he whispered involuntarily. "He must die by my hands."

Antoth did not question the thought. It rested inside him with undisputed certainty. This man was dangerous. He would have to die before Antoth could fulfill his dream of empire. But first he would claim his prize. He concentrated once again on this rich source and a name came to him which caused him to smile. He knew now where the power he needed existed. It was a place familiar to him, a small village nestled among the mountains dividing his realm from the eastern sea. He set about gathering his discs, hoping the talismans would provide him enough energy to make his journey. Once he fed from them he would be on his way. He was going to Axum.

4
DJIBOUTI

Changa sat up in his bunk and winced. He looked at his shoulder, the muscle and bone wrapped tight in heavy gauze. He was healing at least; there was no hint of blood seeping though as it had been days before. The Nuba arrow that struck him weeks before had not only been on fire but was poisoned. Panya's fast work saved his life once again. The days after their flight from Mogadishu was mostly a feverish blur to him, nightmares filled with images of Zakee's funeral and the Tuareg's assault on the Nuba archers. He stood just as helpless in his dreams as he did in life, watching his friends taken away from him just as he watched his father die many years before.

"Changa, sit up," Panya said.

Changa emerged from his half sleep and sat up. Panya handed him a gourd of water. She sat beside him, her face bunched in concern.

"How are you?" she asked.

"Better," he replied. "Where are we?"

Panya frowned. "Djibouti."

Changa smirked. He knew well why Panya scowled. Djibouti was not a place Changa preferred to dock. Because of its close proximity to Aden and its access to the Ethiopian highlands it had been an important city under the Axumite rulers. But time had changed the once important port. Now the anchorage was a shadow of its former self, a place that embraced all the vices of men.

"We won't be here long," Changa assured her. "It's the closest point to Axum. We'll be on our way quickly."

"We won't be going anywhere for a while yet," Panya said. "You are not fully healed. You have at least another week. The Nuba's poisons are potent. It will take time to get it out of your system."

Changa lay back onto his bunk. "So be it. I am in your hands."

Panya looked into his eyes. "Your body heals, but what about the rest of you?"

Changa looked away. "It is what it is. We mourn our losses and we move on."

"It was the right thing to do," Panya said.

"Yes, of course it was."

They sat silent for a moment then Panya left his cabin. Changa sat up, rubbing his chin and agitating his shoulder wound. It was the right thing to do, but was it the best thing? Would the Tuareg have left him to fight alone against such odds? Of course he wouldn't have. He would have come to his aid and fought by his side, no matter the odds. It was his debt he was determined to pay. As far as Changa was concerned there was never a debt owed. He gave to the Tuareg what Belay had given to him.

"I'd forgotten what a vile place Djibouti is," Mikaili said.

The gruff navigator entered the cabin unannounced.

"How are you?" he asked.

"Good," Changa replied.

"Excellent! As soon as you recover from your scrape we can be on our way."

Changa was grateful for Mikaili's words.

"So you are now suddenly anxious to go back to the church? You're a few years late."

Mikaili touched his cross. "When God calls one answers. There was a purpose in my wanderings."

"Did that purpose have anything to do with looting and pillaging?"

"Of course not! I could not help my circumstances. Luckily I survived my trials and was able to return home. That is until I met you and was lured into a different type of looting and pillaging."

"Leave me be," Changa said, a genuine smile on his face. "As soon as I'm able we'll go ashore and head to Axum. Is there anyone you know that can facilitate our journey?"

Mikaili folded his arms across his chest and smiled. "Of

course I do. I'll go ashore and make the arrangements."

"Take the…" Changa stopped mid-sentence.

"I will take two of the baharia with me," Mikaili finished. "Djibouti can be dangerous but not to someone who knows her ways."

"We will wait on your return," Changa said.

Changa rested for the next three days under Panya's constant care. By the fourth day he was feeling much better, the stiffness gone from his arm and the pain a dull throb. But another worry occupied his mind. It had been three days since Mikaili went into Djibouti to make arrangements for their journey. He had not returned.

When Panya entered his cabin on that day he was on his feet, dressed and armed.

"What are you doing?" she asked. "You're still healing."

"Where's Mikaili?" he asked. "Has he returned?"

"No."

"And you don't find that strange?"

"I assumed he was taking longer because he knows this sewer."

"Don't assume," Changa growled.

Panya glared at Changa. "I am not Mikaili. Don't handle me that way."

"I'm sorry," Changa replied. "Get your weapons. We're going ashore. I've already lost two friends. I'm not going to lose another."

Changa strode from the cabin, Panya following close behind.

"You don't know if something's wrong."

Changa emerged on deck and the baharia looked at him in unison. Nafari was at his side instantly.

"Any word from Mikaili?"

"No," Nafari replied. "I fear he may be in trouble."

Changa turned and looked at Panya.

"I'll get my weapons," she said.

Panya went below deck as Changa ordered Nafari to prepare

a boat to take them ashore. Other baharia asked to go as well but Changa refused. He wasn't about to risk anyone else.

"Nafari, I want the cannons loaded and the broadsides facing the city. If we're not back in two days start firing until we return."

"Yes, bwana," Nafari answered.

Panya returned with her sword and whip and they climbed into the boat. Changa rowed while Panya sat at the bow nervously looking back to Changa then to the city.

"This is not smart, Changa," she warned.

Changa didn't answer. When they reached the shallows he jumped into the dingy water and pulled the boat ashore. A throng of beggars ran towards him but halted when Changa's eyes met theirs. They scattered, glancing over their shoulders in fear and anger.

"So, what we do now?" Panya asked.

"We ask questions," Changa replied.

He proceeded to the docks. Groups of dingy men gathered about the various vessels, cutting glances at Changa and especially at Panya as they moved down the dilapidated structure. Changa began to realize how futile his search would be; he'd let his emotions guide him into this situation.

"You seek the old man from your ship, do you not?" a male voice spouted.

Changa spun to his right to face a thin man draped in plain white clothing, his head covered by a jewel cap. He smiled hauntingly.

"Who are you?" Changa demanded.

The man waved Changa's question away. "It doesn't matter. He surprised us; he fought hard for an old Axumite. Some of us were injured. I'm afraid our vigorous subdual resulted in some injuries on his part as well."

Changa punched the man in the face. He fell on his butt, his eyes wide. He moved his mouth to speak and Changa kicked him in the face. The crowd moved in to watch this sudden outbreak among them but Panya brandished her sword and whip.

Changa grabbed the man's shirt and lifted him from the dock.

"Where is Mikaili?" he shouted.

The man sputtered and spit up blood. "You're crazy!"

Changa slapped him across the face. "Where's Mikaili?"

The man's eyes glazed for a moment before he shook his head then blinked his eyes. His anger emerged over his pain.

"He's a dead man!" he spat.

"Then so are you!" Changa yelled.

Changa stood and lifted the man over his head and walked to the edge of the dock.

"Wait, wait!" the man exclaimed.

Changa lowered the man. "I'll ask you one more time, where is Mikaili?"

"I don't know! My task is to deliver the message and arrange the meeting, that's all!"

Changa frowned. "Then you are no use to me."

Changa lifted the man over his head again.

"I can take you to him!" the man squealed.

Changa dropped him on the dock. He knelt close to the man.

"Don't toy with me. You are a dead man until I get my friend back. Do you understand?"

The man nodded then winced.

"Good." Changa yanked the man to his feet. "Let's go."

The man stumbled down the dock. Changa followed and Panya fell into step.

"That was harsh," she whispered. "He could be leading us into an ambush."

"He won't, because he knows he'll be the first one to die," Changa replied. "Either I'll kill him or they will. He has a better chance of living helping us."

"Will you kill him?" Panya asked.

"I don't know yet," Changa replied.

They followed the messenger through Djibouti's chaotic market into a section of town Changa would have otherwise avoided. Ragged stone buildings lined a narrow dirt street, the stench of raw sewage was sickening. The messenger halted then turned to Changa and Panya.

"I must walk ahead alone," he said. "My contact will not show if he sees me with you. That is not part of the plan."

Changa took out a throwing knife. "Do you know what this is?"

The man's eyes widened. "Yes."

"If you betray us it will be in your back."

The man nodded then shuffled away. Changa tensed as the man rapped on the door then sprang from his hiding place, Panya running close behind.

The door creaked open.

"Assad, what are you doing back so soon?"

Assad had no time to answer. Changa shoved the man into the building. Assad fell over the man who answered the door. Changa leaped over both of them, Damascus in one hand, throwing knife in the other. He quickly scanned the room and his anger rose. Five men sat around a table consumed in a game of mancala. On the opposite side of the room bare chested workers stacked boxes of goods, probably stolen. In the back of the room Mikaili lay strewn on the floor, his eyes half open, his face bruised and clothes bloody. Two men sat on either side of him, a grim faced duo that sneered at the Ethiopian as they swigged cups of some unknown brew.

Changa's knife was already out his hand before the men noticed his abrupt intrusion. The blade sank into the face of the man sitting closest to Mikaili and he tumbled from his seat. The men at the table sprang to their feet as they pulled their scimitars free from their ragged sashes. Changa sprinted at them.

"Protect Mikaili!" he yelled at Panya before plunging into chaos. He barely noticed Panya run by as he sliced at the five with his sword. The men stumbled away, giving Changa the room he needed. He grabbed the table in his left hand then raised it before him just as the bandits regained their senses and attacked. Dull blades thudded against the worn wood, breaking it up into splinters.

Changa flung the remaining table at them and came in swift behind the flying wood. One bandit went down with a slash to the belly; another screamed as the Damascus plunged in his thigh. The third batted the table away from his face only to meet Changa's snarling visage as he stabbed the man in the throat. A scimitar flashed by Changa's head, nicking his ear. Changa ducked and stabbed blindly; his efforts rewarded by a short cry.

The distraction of the third attacker gave the two table mates time to unite. As Changa turned to face them they both ran at him, blades ready. Nine beaded strips of leather appeared suddenly across one of the attackers' face, gripping into his flesh and spinning him around. He fell; his image replaced in Changa's view by Panya's angry visage. His eyes remained on her long enough to see her stab the man with her blade before he turned his full attention on his remaining foe.

The man was enthusiastic but unskilled. Changa patiently deflected his attack until fatigue slowed his blows. He dodged a weak thrust then stepped into the man's attack, punching him in the face with his left hand. The bandit's arms fell immediately to his sides as consciousness fled his mind, his sword falling from his hand just before he crashed backwards into the pile of shattered wood that used to be his gaming table.

Changa sheathed his sword and strode to the back of the room. Panya had returned to Mikaili. She was busy with her herb bag, mixing a concoction as he approached.

"How is he?" Changa called out.

"Bad," Panya replied. "These bastards had no intention returning him alive. They were toying with him."

"I suspected as much," Changa answered. He shoved the body of one of the guards aside and knelt close to his friend.

"We're here, old man," he whispered.

"You're damned late," Mikaili managed to whisper back.

"Harsh words from a future priest," Changa chided.

"Don't you two ever stop?" Panya said.

Changa moved to lift Mikaili but Panya raised her hand.

"He's too weak," she said. "We'll have to keep him here for

at least a day."

Changa frowned at the notion of staying in the dilapidated building that long. He scanned the room and noticed a group of workers cowering before a stack of boxes.

"All of you!" he shouted. "Come here!"

The men cut their eyes at the door then back at Changa. Changa raised his throwing knife then cut his eyes at the door as well. The workers' shoulders slumped in unison. They rose and trudged to Changa.

"Get those bodies out of here, and then come back. I'll have more work for you. Don't worry, you'll be paid."

Changa reached into his pouch and gave each man a silver coin. They grinned as they happily dragged the dead bandits from the building. They returned moments later, too soon for Changa's taste. He chose two of the men, a short stocky brute with a crooked smile and a tall lean fellow whose eyes seemed locked in a perpetual squint. Changa took off his bracelet and handed it to them.

"Go to the harbor. There are three dhows anchored away from the shore. Take a boat to the smallest dhow and show them this bracelet. Can you do this?"

The men nodded their heads then ran for the door. Panya motioned the others to her.

"Can you read?" she asked.

One of the men, a stout fellow with a solemn face raised his hand.

"I can."

"Are there writing instruments here?"

"No," the man replied. "These brutes were not much for sending notes."

"Then you'll have to remember what I say." Panya recited a list of herbs and medicines she needed. The man nodded attentively then took the money she gave him.

"I will return soon," he said.

"You better," Changa threatened.

"There is no need to bully me, *bwana*," he responded. "It has been a long time since I had a chance to do a good thing."

The man bowed and went on his way. Mikaili had managed to sit up, Panya doing what she could with what little she had. Changa went out into the street, partly in anticipation of his men arriving at their hovel, partly to discourage any allies of the men he'd just killed from any retaliation. A pall suddenly fell over him as he thought of Zakee and the Tuareg. Both men would have come to his aid, Zakee taking command of the dhows while the Tuareg stood where he stood, guarding them from any intruders that might come his way. Panya had stepped in admirably, returning to her warrior roots. But they were missed. And now with Mikaili returning to finally fulfill his vows Changa felt as if he was losing his mooring. Nafasi was doing an admirable job learning navigation from Mikaili; he was probably better than any baharia along the Swahili Coast. The *Kazuri* sailors were good fighters before they sailed from Sofala two years ago. The experience from their confrontations across the Spice lands made them as formidable as any warriors anywhere. Yet Changa felt exposed. His family was falling apart and sometimes he wondered if he should continue to hold it together. The time was drawing near that he put aside his excuses and set about fulfilling the promise he made in his youth. But was he ready?

One of the workers appeared around the bend with a contingent of *Kazuri* baharia bearing crossbows and supplies. They smiled when they saw Changa, some of them waving as if they were at the end of a casual outing. Changa waved them over.

"Sulemani and Manani, you two keep watch. The rest of you come inside."

The baharia followed Changa into the building. No orders needed to be given; they set about cleaning the large building as they would a warehouse selected for storage. Panya's errand boy returned soon afterwards, his arms filled with the items she requested.

Panya took the items one by one, making sure everything was correct. Once she was done she looked up at him and smiled.

"You did well," she said.

"Thank you misses," he replied.

"What is your name?" Changa asked him.

"Embaye," he answered.

"How would you like to work as Panya's helper?"

Panya glanced at Changa and he shrugged.

"You could use the help, can't you?"

"Yes I can," she answered. "But what of you? Mikaili is in no condition to find us guides to Axum."

"You wish to go to Axum?" Embaye's eyes brightened.

"Yes," Changa said. "Mikaili was securing us transportation and guides before he was kidnapped."

"I'm not dead, you know," Mikaili interjected. "I can still… oww!"

He rubbed his head where Panya hit him.

"You are not doing anything until I say so."

"Earn your pay," Changa told Embaye. "I'd like to be on the way in a few days."

Embaye bowed. "A few days are all I need, bwana."

Changa tossed Embaye a bag of coins. "Spend it wisely."

Embaye peered into the bag and grinned. "This should be more than enough, bwana."

He bowed and trotted for the door.

"You know you'll never see him again, don't you?" Mikaili said. He quickly covered his head for protection.

"He'll be back," Changa said. "He's an honest man."

Mikaili snorted then grimaced. "There's no such thing as an honest man in Djibouti."

"I guess we'll find out," Changa said.

By nightfall he was beginning to think Mikaili was right. A humid night settled on the city, making the warehouse hot and uncomfortable. The baharia prepared meals outside the stuffy building to keep the temperature down. Changa wandered about outside, becoming more and more agitated with each passing minute.

The baharia were preparing for sleep when a commotion in the darkness caught their attention.

"Bwana Changa," someone shouted. "I have returned!"

Embaye emerged from the void followed by a group of men. They were shirtless, their lean bodies glistening with sweat. They all appeared similar; the curled hair draped on their head like a thick curtain ending square with their jaws. Their dark skin and narrow features were similar to the Ethiopians but there was a fire in their eyes that suggested a less civilized origin. Changa rested his hand on the hilt of his Damascus; the baharia did the same.

"Please bwana, do not be alarmed," Embaye said. "You asked me to bring you guides and I have."

Mikaili grunted. "You could have done better. You could have done much better."

Changa deferred to his navigator. "Who are they?"

"Afar," Mikaili spat.

The men shifted, their eyes locked on Mikaili. Embaye spoke to the men in a language Changa didn't understand and they stepped away.

"Bwana Mikaili, you should be careful of what you say," Embaye warned.

"I'll tell you what I know about the Afar," Mikaili said. "They are bandits, every last one of them. They'll lead us out into that desert hole of theirs then rob us of everything we have before they castrate us and leave us for dead."

"That may be true of some, but not all," Embaye said. "You cannot paint a whole people with the colors of those who stray."

"He sounds more like a priest than you," Changa commented. "I've known Mikaili quite some years, Embaye. He's a mean old man but he's guided me and my baharia across the world. Why should I believe you over him?"

"It is not coincidence that I sound like a priest," Embaye said. "It is because I am." He reached into his shirt and extracted a silver cross similar to the one Mikaili wore.

Mikaili sat up, his eyes wide. "Brother, I am sorry."

Embaye waved his hand. "It is understandable, brother. I don't appear as I should. Jibuuti is not a place for the faithful. One must hide his faith to teach it. The Afar are some of my students. Their love of God outweighs that of their brethren."

"I've seen men lose their so-called faith for a dented gold piece," Changa said. "I need something more than faith before I risk my life."

"I believe him," Mikaili said. "Is that good enough?"

"No," Changa replied. "You're wounded."

"I want to go home, Changa," Mikaili fussed. "Embaye says the Afar can lead us there. I'll go with them. You can do what you want."

Changa looked at Panya for support but she said nothing.

"I assure you, bwana Changa, you are in the best of hands," Embaye said.

Changa folded his arms across his chest. "We'll go to Axum then, but only when Mikaili is fit to travel." He gave Embaye a hard look.

"Our lives are in your hands, priest."

Embaye smiled. "No bwana Changa. Our lives are in God's hands."

5

ANTOTH RETURNS

I will make my hands mountains and crush them,
I will swallow their herds.
They will scatter before me like locusts,
I will consume them like fire.
Despair will spread before me like the coming of night,
Ranu will hide her face and share her light with them no more.
I am the bringer of death,
They will know me like kin.

-Antoth's Promise

Antoth sat shirtless in the chariot, the golden falcon talisman warm against his healing skin. Gilded bracelets stacked both arms from his wrist to his elbows. Atop his head sat a crown of gold and ivory, lapis lazuli beads swaying before his face with the rhythm of the chariot. The back of the charioteer blocked his vision of the ragged army marching before him, which for Antoth was a comfort. The men of this age were fragile, their thin bodies like wisps of grass. They struggled to live in a land of sand and shrubs, slaves to their paltry goat and sheep herds, constantly hunting patches of grass to feed them and in turn, feed themselves. The thought that this was the legacy of his people sickened him. Yet, this was the weapon the gods gave him and he would wield it as best he could.

Weeks ago he set out on his quest, moving from crypt to crypt gathering his talismans to marshal his strength. Some he found as he left them, hidden away in secret tombs buried under the sand. Others had been desecrated; the tombs lay open like a hapless beast, its innards strewn across the land. His anger knew no bounds; those he found resulted in the gruesome death of those who possessed them. Others were too far for him to claim, too distant from his prize. Despite his collection the source hidden in Axum still beckoned. With its power his full strength would be restored. Then he would set about building an empire greater than the one he ruled before, a kingdom that would rival that of the gods themselves. And when he was ready, he would take his war to their sacred halls.

The charioteer turned to face him.

"Master, there is something up ahead."

Antoth stood. He towered over the man, his massive size partly that of his people and partly due to the power he held within. He looked over his front line and a smile came to his face. So there were people of this land who possessed spirit.

The army stretched along the undulating horizon for at least one thousand strides. The soldiers wore cotton cloth cloaks over chainmail, the bright sunlight reflecting from their conical helmet. They stood three ranks deep, flanked on either side by cavalry mounted on small but sturdy-looking horses. The commanders were positioned on a nearby hill, surrounded by more cavalry and soldiers.

"Who are they?" Antoth asked his servant.

"They are Makurians," he answered. "They are formidable warriors."

Antoth smirked. "We shall see. Sound the war drums."

The charioteer dropped the reins and shuffled to a huge drum beside him. He grasped the cloth covered batons then beat slowly on the camel skin drumheads. This was not a call to arms, at least not the way most armies would do so. Antoth had no time to drill these weak ones into an efficient fighting unit, so he had to rely on other means. As the drum sound traveled to the ears of his army, their bodies stiffened. Their pace became rigid, their movements spasmodic. Antoth was truly master over them, the drum beat triggering a hypnotic state that gave him full control over his ragged minions. The charioteers fell back behind the cover of the vanguard, working their way to the right flank. A quick assessment of the approaching army revealed they possessed no chariots, giving Antoth a tactical advantage. On the other hand, they were well armed, giving them the advantage against his ill equipped troops.

Antoth commanded his men forward. They advanced silently, their actions controlled by his commands. Archers emerged from the ranks of their adversaries, a tactic Antoth did not expect. The first volley fell on his men and many faltered, taken down by the heavy downpour. But Antoth was prepared for the second volley. He raised his left hand and the wind stirred, the dust rising in small whirlwinds between the armies. Before the archers could release their second volley the tempests spun among them, stinging their eyes and filling their mouths and ears. His men ran through the maelstrom, oblivious to the blinding sand. They smashed into the ranks, swinging their swords and stabbing with their spears, driven by a delirium planted in their minds by Antoth. Their fury forced the Makurians to commit their reserves, a move Antoth anticipated. He sent the chariots forward, the four wheeled wagons rambling toward the right flank of the Makurian line. The Makurians responded with their cavalry, hundreds of armored riders with lances and shields swinging right to meet the cavalry advance. Antoth dropped his hold on his warriors and concentrated on the mobile battle. They were committed now; they would fight for their lives because they had to. The struggle for the right flank would determine the battle. He extended his presence into each charioteer, guiding the archers to shoot the riders mounts from under them as the lancers slayed the fallen knights. The chariots formed a solid wall that the horses would not breach. They mingled in confusion as the archers killed the riders with their powerful short bows. The Makurian flank faltered and the charioteers advance to complete the surrounding maneuver. The Makurian warriors sensed defeat and pulled away, dropping their weapons and holding up their hands in defeat. Such weak men, Antoth thought. In his time men fought to the death, for they knew what defeat meant for them and their families. These men capitulated easily, preferring life as a slave than an honorable death. Antoth planned to honor their wishes.

The surviving Makurians were gathered together, surrounded by Antoth's army. The wounded were immediately killed; he had no time for stragglers. He stood before the defeated flanked by his guard. These men were not drugged like the others; they had seen his power and given their loyalty to him freely. They lead another group of men who carried large barrels on their shoulders.

"You fought valiantly, Makurians," Antoth lied. "Your families need not be ashamed of your efforts. But you have been defeated and you belong to me, as do your families."

Antoth removed his crown. "But let it not be said that Antoth the Humble is not without compassion. Join me on my quest. Stand beside me and reap the reward of my success. We will march across this land and destroy every army before us. Axum is my goal; make it yours, too."

Antoth fell silent, letting his words sink in. He waved his hand and the barrel bearers came forward.

"If you wish to follow me, step forward and drink with us." He walked to the nearest barrel and held out his hand. A servant rushed to his side then handed him a golden goblet, its rim circled with precious stones. Antoth put his goblet below a barrel spigot then watched as a thick red liquid poured into it. He drank it fully then wiped away the residue on his cheek.

"Come, my new brothers! Drink with us and seal the bond of victory!"

The captured Makurians trudged to the barrels, each cupping their hands to catch their portion of the elixir. Antoth looked at them, ignoring the range of emotions on their faces before they took the drink. He knew what they would experience; a thick, sweet concoction that would sooth as it oozed down their throats. He watched as each man sat where they stood as the elixir took effect. Emotion slowly drained from their faces; by the time the last of them drank those that indulged before them were completely under the effect of Antoth's brew. Their memories were erased completely. They were empty vessels waiting to be filled.

Antoth's disciples, those who had willingly chosen to follow him, led the child-like men away to administer other drinks and salves that would transform them into loyal warriors. It was another distasteful procedure, but necessary for his plans. He had no idea what to expect once he reached Axum so he was determined not to arrive alone. The city might have to be taken and he would be prepared to do so.

"Remember Mfumu's Son."

The statement interrupted his musing and forced a deep frown on his face. The essence of the captive spirit lingered, forcing its purpose into his mind. Who was this man that instilled such wrath in him? Since his resurrection he'd encountered no being worthy of such hatred…and fear. The revelation disgusted him. Fear was an emotion that never entered his consciousness until now. This spirit within him was corruption, a spectral plague that needed to be purged. But not now. He still was not strong enough to exist without its life-force. Not until he obtained the source at Axum could he rid himself of this tainted being and its fearful master. He watched his disciples indoctrinating his new army, his mind resolved. He would take Axum and he would claim his prize. If this Changa must die for him to do so, then so be it.

6
AXUM

Embaye's Afar were true to their word. The safari across the arid desert was uneventful, if travel through the desert could be called such. They emerged into the rocky highlands weary yet relieved. The damp air felt good against Changa's dry skin and the subsequent rain was like a blessing. He was tired, but it was good to see the look on Mikaili's face as they traversed the road as it twisted through the hilly landscape. His eyes sparkled like a child's, his mouth curved in a wide smile.

Changa worked his way over to his friend.

"So this is home?" he asked.

"Yes it is, and now that I'm back I wonder why I left," Mikaili replied. "I have seen some magnificent sites in my travels and done some amazing things but nothing compares to home."

Changa smiled but melancholy lurked inside him. He had no such memories of home. Whatever joy he experienced in his short life there was marred by the image of his father's execution and his family's separation. He had found his home on the sea with his crew. The land held no such joy for him.

Though they entered the highlands they were still days away from Axum. They replenished supplies in a small village and took their rest in a grove of trees not far from the road. The next day they continued on, their spirits lifted by fresh supplies and fair weather.

Axum came into view as the sun eased into the western horizon. Centuries ago it had been the center of a flourishing kingdom of the same name that spanned from the northernmost cataracts of the Nile to the shores of the Red Sea. That was long ago; now the city languished in isolation bordered by two hills and two quiet streams on either side. Stelae towered before them as they approached from the east, tall monoliths raised by the once powerful kings that ruled the land. The city existed as the spiritual heart of the land now known as Ethiopia.

Changa was glad he'd come. There was a sense of serenity in the place and it was a welcomed respite from the sea. The real prize was the look on Mikaili's face. He'd never seen the old man so happy; his face glowed like a boy in love for the first time. Panya came close to him and grasped his hand.

"This is a city of great spirit," she said. "Oya respects it."

"There is something about it," Changa agreed. "Maybe we'll stay for a time. We need the rest."

"I agree," Panya answered.

"We will go to the Covenant Church," Embaye shouted. "I have matters to attend to first. Afterwards we will find you all lodging. I thank you for accompanying us."

Mikaili joined them as they entered the city. "Thank you for coming, Changa. I don't know what has become of my blood family. I have been away for so long. I'm happy that I will have my new family with me."

"I wish we all could be here," Changa said.

"We are," Mikaili answered. "I'm sure Zakee is with us in spirit."

"And what of the Tuareg?" Panya asked.

"I haven't given up on him," Mikaili replied. "It will take more than a few thousand mercenaries to stop him."

Changa shrugged. "You are beginning to sound like a priest. All this optimism is turning my stomach."

"Not even you can turn my mood today, Changa," Mikaili said with a smile. "Though if you continue I'll make sure you sleep with the asses if you wish to act like one."

The mood slowly changed as they neared the city. As the villages grew closer they met groups of armed men occupying the road, some small, others large. Though they showed no malice, Changa knew this was no good sign.

"Someone is at war and they have called for support," he said that night before the fire. Panya nodded in agreement. Embaye and Mikaili looked at each other nervously then at Changa.

"Is there something you two would like to share?" he

asked.

"Axum is a sacred city," Mikaili said. "Long ago it was the capital of a great empire that bore its name. During that time it also became the capital of our faith. It possesses one of the most sacred items of our belief, the Ark of the Covenant. It has always been believed that one day someone…or something would try to claim the Ark for its own."

"The day may have come," Embaye finished.

Changa rubbed his chin. "What makes you think that? Men fight for many different reasons. We may be caught up in another local dispute."

Embaye shook his head. "No, this is greater than that. See these warriors?"

Embaye waved his hand around. "They are of different kingdoms and different tribes. Some of them are bitter rivals. Yet they sit together breaking bread. There are only two reasons that we as a people would unite; for our faith and for our land. As far as I know we are not being invaded."

"Changa may be right," Panya said. "I have traveled much of this world and I know you have enemies to the north. They want your land and they wish to convert you from your faith."

Embaye's face became somber. "I have a feeling this is something more. I can't explain it."

"Well, we won't discover it tonight," Changa said. "Best we get some rest. We'll arrive in Axum tomorrow and the mystery will solve itself."

As he lay on his blanket under the star filled night, Changa secretly shared Embaye's misgivings but for a different reason. A familiar feeling was growing in him as well, a warning of a threat that had plagued him since he fled his homeland. There was a tebo nearby.

Changa's sleep was brief and restless. He rose to a gray sky, a sign of the coming rains. Breakfast was a silent affair of bread and fruit then they were on the road again for Axum. By midday the ancient city came into view. The city rested among groves of trees, its stone buildings and wide avenues an image of its former glory.

More stele rose high over the surrounding buildings, monuments of the great kings that once ruled the land from the city itself to the ocean shores of Mogadishu and Djibouti and as far north to the Nile.

"We shall go to the church," Embaye said. "The priests will tell us what is going on."

Though the city was surrounded by various armies its interior held only residents and pilgrims. There was one building however that drew the attention of the martial elements. A solitary church stood near the city's center, its blue dome rising over the thick stone wall surrounding it. Armed guards traced the wall, their faces stern and their eyes alert.

"What's in there?" Changa asked.

Both Embaye and Mikaili looked at Changa.

"The Ark of the Covenant," they said in unison.

"The Ark?" Changa was confused. "What does this have to do with anything?"

Mikaili frowned and Embaye shook his head.

"Probably nothing, but possibly everything," Embaye said.

They approached the gate entrance and were immediately confronted by the guards. A burly soldier with thick shoulders and a painful scowl stepped before them, his hand raised.

"No one enters the Church of the Ark," he grumbled.

Embaye reached into his shirt and extracted his cross. The man's narrow eyes opened slightly wider then he gave Embaye a curt bow.

"Tell my brothers that Embaye has returned from Djibouti," Embaye instructed. "I have friends as well."

The man nodded again and waved over another soldier.

"Tell them yourself," he said. "My man will escort you."

Embaye turned to them, his eyes focused on Changa. "Please wait here. I will only be a moment."

Embaye and the soldier passed through the gate and entered the Church. Changa folded his arms across his chest as Panya came to his side.

"What do you know of this ark?" he asked her.

"It is a sacred symbol of Christians," she said.

"I know a few Christians," he replied. "I never heard them speak of an ark."

Mikaili interrupted them with a grunt. "Just because you never heard of it doesn't mean it doesn't exist. As you can see, it does."

"So tell me, priest to be, what is this ark and why would an army come to take it. It is made of gold and jewels?"

"No. It is much more valuable than that. It's priceless."

Changa rolled his eyes. "Everything has a price."

"A merchant would say that. A merchant will sell anything, but that doesn't mean everything can be given a value. You had a price once, did you not?"

Changa glared at Mikaili. He usually took his insults lightly but there was weight behind his words this time. Apparently his questioning of this ark had slighted his friend.

"So you were telling us about the ark," Panya said, apparently sensing the tension between the two.

Mikaili's eyes lingered on Changa a bit longer before he continued. "After Moses led the Hebrews from Egypt he was called by the Lord to receive the Ten Commandments, the laws by which they were to live. An ark was constructed to contain the stone tables. The Word of the Lord possessed his power, sometimes acting as a weapon against the enemies of His people.

"Many years later the land of the Hebrews was ruled by a wise man named Solomon. Our land was ruled by the beautiful Queen of Sheba, who was intrigued by the stories she heard of this man. She traveled to his kingdom and was enamored with him. After she returned to her kingdom she bore him a child. That son returned to his father's land and asked for the Ark as a gift in honor for the love between his mother and the king. His request was granted, and so the Ark has been among us since then. Others have come to claim it but we have defended it as our right to claim it."

Changa rubbed his chin skeptically although he did sense

some truth in Mikaili's words. He felt different in the presence of this building, as if an invisible force embraced him and eased his weight.

The doors of the Church opened and Embaye emerged followed by three other men. They were all draped in elaborate clothing with large jeweled crosses hanging from their necks. The soldiers snapped to attention as they reached the gate. Mikaili bowed in their presence; Changa and Panya remained standing.

"These are the priests of the Covenant," Embaye said. "I told them of you and they wished to see you."

Changa grinned. "It seems you are more important than I thought, Mikaili."

Embaye shook his head. "Not him, Changa. They wish to see you."

The priests talked among themselves as they studied Changa, Embaye occasionally joining in. The eldest of the priest then stepped to Changa, placing his hands on the Bakonga's shoulders then closing his eyes.

"What is he doing?" Changa asked.

"He's praying for you," Mikaili answered. "Close your eyes."

Changa closed his eyes and bowed his head like the others. He felt something placed around his neck and opened his eyes. A cross similar to the one Mikaili and Embaye wore dangled from his neck. Changa held the object and frowned.

"Another talisman?" he said.

"Much more than that," Embaye said. "Much more."

Changa shrugged. "Tell him I said thank you. So when does this priesthood ceremony take place?"

"There will be no ceremony until the Enemy has been defeated," Embaye said.

"I think it's time you told us what is going on here," Changa demanded.

"Word has come from the north of a massive army marching in this direction. No one knows who they are. They came from the desert and are led by a mysterious man called simply the Enemy."

"Why is that a concern to us?" Mikaili asked. "Whatever or whoever this Enemy is, he will never make it past the Makurians."

A worried looked took over Embaye's face. "He already has. In fact, many Makurians have joined him."

The news of the Makurian defeat seemed to shake Mikaili. "Then there is nothing to stop him from reaching Axum."

"No," Embaye replied.

"So this is the reason the kingdoms are gathering," Changa said.

"We believe he comes for the Ark," Embaye said. "It is said he possesses powers long forgotten, and that power is fueled by a collection of talismans. He has no regard for our faith. He may see the Ark as another relic to be collected to add to his power."

"He cannot take the Ark!" Mikaili exclaimed. "The Lord will not allow it. We won't allow it!"

"I agree, my brother," Embaye said. "But that does not mean he will not try."

"I came to see an induction, not fight a war," Changa said. "I'm sorry, Mikaili but I think we will leave. I would suggest you come with us."

Mikaili's eyes went wide. "Are you mad? I know why I came back now and why I insisted you come with me. We are here for a reason."

Changa looked at Mikaili and his frown deepened. Mikaili was truly angry with him.

"That may be what you believe," Changa replied. "I have no desire to participate in this fight."

"Changa, let's think about this before we decide," Panya said. She'd been silent throughout the conversation.

"There's nothing to think about. We're leaving."

Panya grabbed Changa's arm and pulled him away. "What is happening to you? Is this how we treat each other now?"

Changa snatched his arm away from her grip. "This is not our fight."

"The Han's emperor was not our fight, neither was

Sharmila's plight, but we fought for them, people who were not of our crew. Now a member of our own wishes our help and you want to walk away. This is not the man I followed from Sofala. This is not the man that I love."

Panya's admission of her feelings was overshadowed by Changa's growing anger.

"We have left a trail of dead brothers across the world," he retorted.

They looked at each other, unsure expressions on their faces.

"I'm staying," Panya finally said. "I will not desert a friend."

She spun and stomped away. Changa watched her, his anger tumbling into a pit of confusion. He trudged back to the group, ignoring Mikaili and Panya's angry stares and the priests' hopeful expressions.

"We will stay, although I'm not sure what good it will do," he said.

The priests grinned and raised their faces and hands to the sky. Mikaili's anger fled and he rushed Changa, wrapping him up in a tight hug.

"I knew you would stay, my brother," he said.

Panya was the only person that remained distant, her expression unchanged. She nodded curtly then marched away to the baharia.

"The priests would like you and your men to augment the church guards," Embaye said. "They are very shorthanded."

Changa nodded, his eyes fixed on Panya. "That's fine. We will stay until your threat has passed."

"Thank you, Changa," Mikaili said. "You are a true brother."

Changa was walking away when Mikaili's last words were uttered. Panya saw him approaching and turned away.

"Come with me," he said as he grabbed her arm.

Panya snatched her arm away and glared at him.

"Come with me…please," he said.

The two walked until they were reasonably alone. Panya turned to face him.

"What do you want?" she asked.

"I did not ask you to take the place of my second," Changa said. "You chose to on your own."

"You needed someone to take the Tuareg's place," she said.

"That may be so, but the Tuareg would never disagree with me in front of anyone."

"I am not the Tuareg."

"That is obvious."

They were quiet for a moment, staring at each other like facing cliffs. After a while Panya's expression softened.

"The past few months have been hard," she said. "We have lost close friends."

Changa nodded. The images of Zakee's funeral and the Tuareg riding away in Mogadishu flashed through his mind.

"This is a good place to rest not only our bodies but our minds. We have not properly grieved."

"And how do we grieve in the midst of a war?" Changa asked.

Panya laid her hand on his shoulder. "This is the moment we have. We must make the best of it."

Changa grasped her hand and felt her warmth. "Will you share my room tonight?"

Panya answered with a smile.

Their moment was interrupted by Embaye.

"The priests have secured lodging for us," he said.

Embaye walked away and they followed.

Panya grasped his hand and squeezed it. Changa smiled at her, but inside an ominous feeling grew stronger. There was no doubt from where it came. He was being hunted again.

7

THE PRIZE

The motley amalgam of men marched silently through the sparse vegetation, undaunted by the hilly rough terrain. Their blank expressions revealed their condition; their minds were not their own. They took no care in preserving themselves, walking into rivers too swift to ford to be washed away, stumbling over stones and breaking bones, tumbling off the edges of steep cliffs without a sound. Despite their continuous losses they were still a massive group, marching relentlessly toward a destination that did not matter to them.

Antoth was very pleased. His new army had conquered every foe in their path and the survivors had swelled his ranks. His spells were much more effective among these newer, weaker men; even his influence among those undrugged was more complete than among his own kind. Still he missed the vigor of the men of his time.

They were closer to his goal. He could feel its power; it was an object possessing a unique force unlike any he'd ever encountered. There was something more to it, a link of some kind that lead to a greater power which he did not recognize. In fact, Antoth encountered a feeling that took him time to interpret, for it was an emotion he'd only seen in others and never in himself. Fear was the word men used and it angered him that this useless sensation invaded his mind. It was no doubt the result of the essence he'd claimed to revive himself, the spirit that clung tenaciously to him no matter how hard he tried to rid himself of it. It remained, droning its only demand into him until its purpose had become almost as important as claiming the prize he sought. He would kill this man Changa, if only to rid himself of the spiritual infection inside him.

Night and day they marched, the attrition growing day by day. After three weeks Antoth willed the army to halt and allowed his sycophants to feed the ragged group. For three days they languished, the stench of the camp preceding them. By the time Antoth stirred his force to motion again the lands before him had been forewarned. The land cleared before them, his army encountering empty villages and towns. Livestock had been slaughtered, fields and crops burned to slow down the advancing horded. It did not matter for it was not needed. They were close; there would be no stopping from this point until they entered Axum.

Antoth was enjoying the entertainment of his lovelier followers when two of his followers appeared before him. They dragged a man between them, a man whose clothing revealed him to be a shepherd. His brown face was battered and he bled from his mouth and nose.

"Give him water," Antoth said. His men looked confused until Antoth glared at them. They placed the man down gently and fetched him water. The man struggled to sit, grimacing as he adjusted himself on the hard grown. When one of the warriors offered him a pitcher of water he waved him away.

"Drink!" the warrior shouted. "My master commands it!"

The man looked into the pitcher then spat blood into it.

"Insolent fool!" the warrior shouted. He struck the man with the pitcher and he tumbled over.

"Leave him be!" Antoth said. He rose from his chariot and the others immediately prostrated before him. The shepherd righted himself, holding his head where the warrior struck him. He opened his eyes and stared at Antoth. The old wizard smelled his fear.

"Do not fear," Antoth said. "I mean you no harm." Antoth had no interest in the shepherd; what drew him was the object hanging from his neck, an elaborate cross held in place by a worn strip of leather.

"What is this you wear?" he asked.

The shepherd clutched the cross in his fist. "Stay away from me, Evil One!"

Antoth grasped the man's hand and squeezed. The shepherd resisted for a moment then opened his hand, his face twisted with pain. Antoth snatched the metal from the shepherd's neck. The metal pulsed with power, a minute amount, but power nonetheless. This was a talisman he was unfamiliar with, but his instincts told him it had something to do with the power he sought. He clinched his fist about the object and cleared his mind to absorb the power within. When he opened them the power was still in the metal. Antoth experienced another emotion he was not familiar with: surprise.

He looked at the shepherd. The man's expression revealed his resolve. He was sure he was going to die. Antoth's warrior approached the man, his sword drawn.

Antoth turned away returning to his chariot.

"Leave him be," he said.

The warrior's confused countenance greeted Antoth as he turned to sit.

"But Master, he insults you!"

"That is his choice," Antoth said. "If you showed as much strength you would probably still be a free man. Dead, but free."

"Go," Antoth told the man. "Go to Axum and tell them that Antoth the Benevolent is coming. Tell them that there are only two things I wish of them; their object of power and their loyalty. It is all I ask."

"They will not bow to you," the shepherd answered.

Antoth smiled. "Then they will die."

8

CHOSEN

Changa sat up suddenly in his cot in terrible pain. A ball of fire burned his stomach and he retched. He tried to stand but his legs gave way and he fell into his own vomit. Never before had he felt such pain. He lay on his back, clutching his stomach.

Panya came to his side, her eyes wide with fear.

"Changa! Changa!" she shouted.

But Changa did not hear her. He was under attack in a way he'd never experienced. There was nothing to grab, no one to confront, just a debilitating pain that bored into his bowels like a jagged knife. Changa could only grit his teeth as the pain burned through him.

The burning sensation suddenly abated. The pain in his abdomen subsided and he opened his eyes. Panya straddled him, rubbing a foul ointment on his chest.

"I'm fine," he said weakly. "Thank you."

Panya dismounted him, clearly exhausted.

"Are you sure?" she panted.

Changa sat up holding his aching stomach. "Yes, I think so, at least for now."

"Do you know…?"

"Tebo." Changa said.

Changa struggled to his feet. He went to the corner where he kept his weapons and began to dress.

"Wait a minute!" Panya shouted. "What are you doing?"

"I'm going," he said.

"Going? Going where?"

Changa looked into her wide, worried eyes. "There is a tebo near. I've felt it since we began this journey. But it's different than before. This one is much stronger."

"So where are you going?"

"I'm going to find it and kill it."

"I'm going with you."

"No!" Changa's pain was replaced by anxiety and worry. "I'm going alone. No one can slay a tebo but me."

"I can help you," Panya pleaded.

"I said no, Panya. This is my fight. No one else dies."

Panya stopped him, her desperate hands grasping his broad shoulders. "You don't know the way and you don't know what waits for you. Let us come with you. Let me come with you!"

Changa grasped her wrists and pulled her to him. Her arms fell around his shoulders and his wrapped tight around her waist. They kissed long and deep.

Changa pulled away. "Sooner or later I will have to confront my hunter. If I cannot face his servants, how can I expect to face him?"

Panya's face became stern. "I am coming with you!"

Changa smiled. "I can't imagine anyone I would want with me more. But I could not take it if I lost you."

"How do you think I feel?" Panya replied. "I've traveled the width and breath of this land. I have been to the far reaches of his world I have never met a man I wish to be with until I met you. I will not lose you."

Reason would not win this argument, Changa realized.

"Please stay, Panya. Please."

Panya held his face, gritting her teeth as her frustration escaped as a hiss between her teeth.

"Come back to me, Changa," she whispered. "Come back to me."

Changa hugged her again then left their room. He walked into the darkness, following the same sensation that warned him of the tebo's proximity. The streets of Axum were empty; the occasional bleat of a restless goat the only sound. He neared the outskirts of the city when a desperate call stopped him.

"Changa, wait!"

It was not Panya. Mikaili rode up to him on the back of an ass. He clambered off the exhausted beast and ran up to Changa.

"Panya told me you were leaving," he said.

"You cannot stop me," Changa replied.

"I'm not going to." Mikaili took off the elaborate cross on his neck.

"I don't know why you think you should do this alone, but I respect your decision. You have never led us wrong, so I suspect that you know what you are doing. But just in case you don't, take this."

"Mikaili, you know I don't…"

"Take it, Changa, please. It will make me feel better."

Changa sighed then accepted the cross. He placed it around his neck with the necklace Panya gave him in the land of the Han. He looked into Mikaili's smiling face.

"Now you are ready," he said.

Changa gave Mikaili a brief hug then proceeded into the darkness. He walked for hours, his only light the weak glow of a half moon. The tebo's sensation led him like a broad path. He followed the feeling across a wide grassy plain and across a slow moving river, undaunted by fatigue or hunger. His entire body and mind was focused on the coming confrontation.

He reached the base of a group of steep hills by midnight. Their slopes were heavily wooded but Changa could sense the way. He also sensed he'd found the adversary's army. The stench of the camp drifted down the slope to his nose. Changa had not considered that he would be among the enemy's camp when he found his nemesis but it did not matter. The fight would be between him and the tebo; the vile creature would kill anyone or anything that tried to claim its prize. Changa was sure there would be no interference. Changa weaved through the sparse forest until reaching the hill summit. Below was the strangest scene he'd ever witnessed. Thousands of men stood on their feet like statues. Their eyes were open, but it was obvious they did not see. A small group of men worked their way through them, stopping to insert spoons of food into the standing men's mouths, like feeding babes. The men chewed absently as they continued to stare into the darkness.

A large tent occupied the center of the bizarre scene, a flickering light revealing moving shapes inside. Changa was again perplexed; the sensation that drew him emanated through the canvas. He'd never known a tebo to reside in a structure. This confrontation was becoming stranger with each moment.

The tent flap suddenly opened. A figure stepped out, a man like Changa had never seen before. His skin was black like obsidian yet glowed with power. Even from a distance Changa could tell he was tall, at least a foot taller than the Bakonga. The man he gazed upon was surely not a tebo, but there was something about him that hinted of an intimate association with such a creature. The man's head turned from side to side as if searching for something, then turned in Changa's direction.

"There you are!" The voice pierced his mind like a spear and Changa stumbled. Cold tendrils dug into his head and Changa fell to his knees.

"You are stronger than I imagined," the voice said. "To kill you would be a waste."

Changa grasped his head and shook it violently. He would not be possessed.

"The one inside me urges me to be done with you, but it is a mindless servant. It does not know your potential, but its master does. That's why it seeks to kill you."

The rigid warriors turned toward him in unison. Their feeders fled as their master strode across the field, followed by an armed contingent. Changa was on his knees, still fighting against the invasion of his mind. The strange man was almost upon him when brightness flooded his head, shattering the dark coils that grasped his thoughts. Changa had experienced this surge before in his life, a mysterious inner force that seemed to appear at his darkest moments. But this time it was accompanied by a stronger force, a presence that continued to surge with every moment. Changa opened his eyes, realizing the source of the well of power. It was Mikaili's cross.

He was standing when the man reached him. The man halted, a smirk coming to his face. His eyes focused on the cross.

"It's like the shepherd's," he said.

"Who are you?" Changa asked.

"I am Antoth. I seek the source of the power of the cross. You will lead me to it."

Changa smirked. "I will not. I have come to kill the creature that seeks me and defend those that you wish to harm."

Antoth laughed and his contingent joined him. "You come alone? I have faced many armies on my march, but never have I faced a madman."

Changa stepped forward, bolstered by the energy surging through him. Antoth's eyebrows raised and he smiled.

"You stand between me and my ambitions, Changa of the Bakongo. It is a shame. You would have made a great champion."

Antoth's sword streaked at Changa's throat. He barely had time to raise his own; the blade met with a force that lifted him off his feet and sent him flying. Changa relaxed his body as he struck the ground on his shoulder then rolled to his feet. Antoth and his minions were running toward him, the warlock's sword raised high. Changa braced himself, spreading his legs in a firm stance, shimsar in one hand, a throwing knife in the other. He noticed Antoth's eyes widen as he lifted the throwing knife and his question of the tebo was answered. The creature was inside the warlock. He had somehow used the foul creature to resurrect himself. But if he lived because of the beast, he could die the same way.

A more sinister situation was forming beyond his immediate assailants. The other warriors advanced toward him, thousands of entranced men to add their steel to the attack. He'd been foolish to go on this safari alone. He'd expected to confront a tebo; instead he was facing down an army. He was in the midst of Antoth's camp so there was nowhere to run. Changa smirked; so it was his time to die. A brief chill of sadness passed through him as he remembered his promise to his mother and sisters, the promise he would not be able to fulfill. The image of his father's execution also appeared, his stern unyielding expression as Usenge struck his head free with the executioner's sword.

"Forgive me, father," he whispered. "I will be with you soon."

Changa threw his knife. The blade spun toward, Antoth,

barely missing the war chief's head and burying into the skull of the man behind him. Changa yelled and leaped at Antoth, his attack furious and lethal. He wove a deadly dance around the warlock, pressing him with powerful slashes while striking down his cohorts with lethal speed. In moments the two stood alone, his men dead or dying around him. The entranced warriors advance slowed, their feet barely moving, their arms sagging as if the weapons they carried had increased in weight. Changa was immersed in his battle with Antoth; he did not notice the cross on his neck gaining luminance. As he raised his sword again beams of light burst from the object, drowning him in light. Changa shielded his eyes and staggered back, swinging wildly in a desperate attempt to defend. The light receded and his eyes cleared to a stunning sight. Antoth's horde emerged from its trance, the men stumbling about, their wide eyes and gaped mouths expressing their confusion. They dropped their weapons and stared in awe at the violent battle taking place among them, a struggle between men far beyond their feeble state. Some sagged to the ground and watched the battle, others stumbled away, eager to be away from the scene. None continued to advance.

If the duo noticed the release of Antoth's horde they did not betray it. Changa concentrated every part of his being on the adversary before him, matching the warlock stroke for stroke with his sword and knife. The man seemed relentless but so was the Bakongo, fueled by the glowing cross about his neck. Antoth's face revealed a different emotion, a mixture of frustration and disgust.

Changa twisted his torso, avoiding a viper-like thrust at his chest. He twisted back, landing a kick into Antoth's stomach that lifted the warlock into the air. He crashed into the ground, his weapons flying from his hands. Antoth scrambled to his feet as Changa advanced for the kill. He traced a pattern into the air and Changa slammed into an unseen barrier. Antoth picked up his weapons and turned to the determined warrior.

Never before had he confronted such a powerful warrior. Although he knew the man drew his power from the talisman, he was astounded that he could contain, let alone control, such power. Such a man could rule empires. In a different time he would have been a dangerous foe. Antoth watched as his spell crumbled against his onslaught. A wild urge flashed in his mind and he suppressed it. The creature inside him hungered for the kill; he was becoming harder to control. Antoth loathed the presence inside him but he still needed it. Unless…

The warlock was on his feet by the time Changa breached the invisible shield. Changa attacked, expecting him to defend himself with his blade. Instead the warlock dropped his guard. Changa's sword pierced his chest and passed through is body. Changa fell into the man, suddenly finding himself face to face with the wizard. The man smiled triumphantly and with his left hand snatched the cross from Changa's neck. Fatigue crashed down on Changa like an avalanche, forcing him to his knees. The wizard pulled himself free from Changa's blade and shouted in triumph as he held the glowing cross. Changa could barely stay upright as he watched the morbid celebration. Still he forced himself to his feet, his Damascus barely gripped in his weak hands.

"Now you will see what I am truly capable of," Antoth hissed. He raised his hands over his head, the cross held in his left palm. Dark clouds appeared in the once clear sky, converging directly over the warlock. They spun, generating lightning that brought day to night and thunder that shook the ground beneath Changa's feet.

"This is the power I craved!" Antoth shouted. "This is the power I deserved!"

Antoth opened his hands. The cross burn so bright Changa had to look away. He brought his hands down suddenly and a lightning bolt followed Antoth's direction, striking Changa's sword. Pain blasted through his body; Changa expected more pain, instead he found his power renewed. He sprang to his feet, ready to renew his battle with Antoth. But the wizard did not stand before him. A mummified husk lay on the ground instead. Behind it stood a massive tebo, its pulsing gray mass barely visible in the darkness. Its mouth open and the tebo screeched his name, the sound cutting through the rumbling thunder. Changa felt no fear. This was a foe he was familiar with. He sheathed his sword and took two throwing knives from his sash. Changa reared back with both arms and threw his knives. They flew from his hands like bolts, tearing through the tebo as easy as blades through cloth. The tebo howled again, this time in pain. Two more knives tore through its torso; the tebo staggered backwards as Changa circled it to receive his knives. This time he did not throw them. He advanced on the wounded beast, hacking at it with incredible speed. The tebo's howl became a long continuous moan as Changa continued his grim work.

When the sound ceased the beast sent to kill him lay in an oozing heap beside the crumbling body of Antoth. Changa's energy seeped away; as fatigue found him once again he noticed brightness out of the corner of his eye. He looked in the direction of the light and saw Mikaili's cross, the pulsing glow bright yet fading. The light diminished and the sky cleared. As the last of the light dispersed Changa stood alone in darkness. There was no army surrounding him; Antoth's sycophants were gone. A feeling of serenity settled upon him, a calmness that formed in his mind. Changa picked up the cross and draped it over his shoulders. He stood, and with his remaining strength, began his return to Axum.

9

Mikaili the Priest

It was a much simpler ceremony than Changa expected. Mikaili approached the other priests garbed in a black robe covering his simple white garb, a short cylindrical cap covering his head. He held a wooden staff capped by a gilded cross which matched the cross hanging from his neck. As he reached the pulpit of the church he knelt before the senior priests and bowed his head. Changa did not understand the words being read and recited but he knew their intent. He absently touched the cross around his neck, the cross given to him by Mikaili that saved his life. Panya touched his arm.

"Our group grows smaller," she whispered.

Changa nodded. At least this was a somewhat peaceful homecoming. It took him two weeks to return to Axum, his safari slowed by his slowly healing wounds. The holy city had become a war camp in his absence as the Ethiopians prepared for Antoth's onslaught. For once his exploits had not preceded his arrival. His subtle coming hid the momentous news he relayed to the Covenant priests. Antoth and his army would not attack. The priests relayed Changa's news to the city's military leaders. At first they scoffed; how could one man defeat an entire army? After another week passed with no attack they dispatched scouts to confirm Changa's word. The scouts returned jubilant. Antoth's army was indeed gone. The Devil had been vanquished.

Mikaili stood and the other priests embraced him. He strode down the aisle, a wide smile on his grizzled face, his arms outstretched.

"Mikaili the priest," Changa announced.

Mikaili embraced Changa with a brotherly hug, surprising the burly Bakongo when he lifted him off his feet.

"Be careful old man!" Changa exclaimed. "You're a priest now, not a strong man."

"I am filled with God's spirit," he said. "I have the strength of ten men!"

"Congratulations, Mikaili," Panya said. They embraced and Panya kissed his cheek.

"Thank you, sister. A lifelong dream has finally been fulfilled. Thank you both."

They left the church together to join the modest feast awaiting them in the church courtyard. It was a day to celebrate Mikaili's ordination, but all eyes fell on Changa.

"I think you are stealing the show," Panya whispered.

"It's not my intention. Today is Mikaili's day."

"You can't blame them. In their eyes you vanquished an army alone, yet you have said nothing of your deed and you've asked for nothing in return."

"I told you what happened. That is enough. Can I enjoy my food now?"

"You should say something," she urged him.

Changa dropped his bread and glared at Panya. He took a swig of wine then stood.

"I have something to say."

Everyone fell silent, their eyes transfixed on him. Mikaili looked at him with bright eyes and a proud smile, an expression that seemed infectious. Changa smiled back.

"Ten years ago I visited Mogadishu and forced an old man back to the sea. One day after we set sail I regretted my decision. He was irritable, mean and challenged my every order and request. Three days after we set sail I was reminded of why I pursued him. Mikaili is the finest navigator that sailed the seas, and I have no doubt that he'll be just as fine a priest."

Changa raised his cup to Mikaili. "I will miss you greatly, my brother."

Mikaili's eyes glistened. "And I, you."

Changa sat and resumed his meal.

"That's not what I expected," Panya said.

"I know," Changa replied.

Later that night Changa lay beside Panya, his eyes open.

They had made love hours before, Panya grateful to have him by her side again. But he was restless. He put on his clothes and left their room, stepping into the warm night. The hazy sky obscured the stars; the hilly horizon was barely visible. He thought of Zakee, the memories bringing a melancholy smile to his face. At the young amir's funeral he'd cursed himself for bringing Zakee back to suffer such a fate. Panya attempted to soothe his pain with words he would not listen to. As he looked into the sky the words finally reached his heart. Zakee had died, but he died fulfilling his duty for his family and his people.

Changa turned to face Panya. The worried look on her face told him he couldn't avoid the conversation any longer.

"Changa, please tell me what is wrong," she said.

Changa smiled at Panya and took her hand.

"I have been running all my life," he said. "I ran from home fleeing Usenge's wrath. I fought in the pits of Mogadishu, running from the specter of death. I ran from Mombasa to avoid a coming war and I fled Sofala because of the tebos. A few weeks ago, beyond those mountains, I decided to stop running. It's time for me to go home."

Panya's eyes widened. "Home to Sofala?"

Changa gripped her hand tighter. "No. Home to Kongo."

Panya suddenly embraced him. He felt a warm tear on his shoulder; he wrapped his arms around her as well.

"If it is time then it is time," she whispered. "I will go with you."

"No," Changa said. "I thought when I returned home I would do so leading an army purchased with my wealth. But I know that it doesn't matter how many men I take with me, in the end it will come down to me and Usenge. I won't have anyone die needlessly on my account."

Panya pulled away from him enough so he could see her determined face.

"I told you in China that I would not take a man as a companion until my head and my heart agreed. I can tell you that now they do. You are my man, Changa Diop. And I will go with you to Kongo."

They kissed, Changa savoring the feeling of certainty between them.

"So what do we do now?" Panya asked.

"First we go back to Sofala. Our brothers have been too long from home. It's time they saw their families and received their share of our bounty."

"And then?"

Changa smiled. He took her hand and together the returned to their humble room, the future as exciting and uncertain as a fresh horizon.

-THE END-

Safari Glossary

Amir – prince

Baharia – sailors

Bwana – Swahili for sir

Dhow – Arabic/Swahili word for ship

Houdah – a carriage positioned on the back of an elephant

Jambiya – a dagger carried by most Yemeni men

Mahout – an elephant driver

Raja – king or prince

Sahib – owner, proprietor

Shamsir – a curved, single edge sword

Shesh – the Tuareg turban and face veil

Takouba – a traditional Tuareg sword

Vijayanagar – City of Victory

The Safari Concludes in 2013!

Changa has braved the eastern seas in search of wealth and adventure. In Changa's Safari: Volume III, Changa begins his final journey. The boy that fled Kongo returns as a man to confront his fears and fulfill his promise. But before he ventures home, there are adventures and challenges in store. The sails are furled and the dhows are docked. Will Changa fulfill his destiny? The answers will be revealed in Volume III!

Amenokal Bazu rushed to the head of the caravan, his camel grunting in protest. Iklan warriors ran beside him, iron allarhs and ayars in hand. The raid had been well timed and well executed. Despite the fact the caravan was guarded by Songhai soldiers, Bazu had expected no problems. The Songhai were good fighters, but weeks in the desert would weakened the strongest men, even Ihagaren.

He sped by the dead Songhai and ignored the piles of goods sprawled in the sand. The first sight of a dead Iklan made him frown; the sight of a slain Ihagaren raised the fire of anger in his breast. By the time he reached the head of the caravan he was seething. He broke through the ring of Iklans, riding toward the man they surrounded. His camel cried out and suddenly he fell to the side. He leaped away from the beast and landed hard in the sand. Bazu cursed as he stood then stomped to his camel. The end of an allarh protruded from the beast. Whoever this man was that would slay such a valuable beast? Bazu would not have time to know; he was going to kill him swiftly.

The amenokal finally turned his attention to the man. He was not a man of the south or the north. To Bazu's surprise he was Ihagaren. Though his robes were ragged, they were those of a noble clan. He did not stand on guard. His posture was almost nonchalant, as if he was out for an evening walk, not surrounded by men about to take his life. Bazu snatched his takouba from his jeweled baldric, eager to be done with this costly distraction. But then he noticed something about the interloper and he slowed his pace. In addition to the takouba in his right hand, a scimitar rested in the folds of his sash. Bazu slowed as the man gripped the scimitar's hilt and slowly extracted it. The man crouched, scimitar held low, takouba held high. Bazu stopped, assuming a similar stance. His mind raced; there was something familiar about this man, something foreboding.

The man remained still. The surrounding Iklans decided the time was right and they rushed by Bazu with a chorus of yells and curses, allarhs lowered and ayars raised. The mysterious Ihagaren met their attack, whirling into them and cutting them down with speed and ferocity. Bazu's eyes widened and he began to back away. The memories he searched for became clear as the last Iklan fell to a scimitar sweep that freed his head from his neck. Long ago, when he was a boy, Bazu knew of a man who fought in such a way, a man whose skills were only matched by his cruelty. He was a man so reviled that despite forging his people into the most powerful clan of the deserts, it was his own who conspired to have him killed.

Their eyes met and Bazu knew. The world spun about him like swirling sand, the only unmoving object the covered man stalking toward him.

"No!" he exclaimed. "It cannot be!"

The man continued to advance, his swords raised. Bazu's mouth went dry with fear, but he still managed to cry out before the man fell upon him.

"Sirrocco!"

Fourteen Writers. Fourteen Artists.
One Unforgettable Anthology

Griots: A Sword And Soul Anthology
Purchase yours today!

For more information visit us at
www.mvmediaatl.com